THE CAST OF CHARACTERS

UPSTAIRS

The parents:

BENJAMIN LASSITER, 65, a self-made man; tough, smart. The "grey eminence" in Boston's City Hall; a power in the state and national party. By the time he was thirty he'd made a fortune. Now, on the eve of Prohibition, he is about to become one of the richest men in America.

MARY LASSITER, 65, ailing but still sharp, incisive and very good company. When her father died, she inherited two million dollars.

The children:

MAUDE LASSITER PALMER, 38, a devoted mother of four and a great beauty. Married to RICHARD, a pleasant, if dull, amateur yachtsman.

EMILY LASSITER BULLOCK, 36, a caustic, covetous beauty. Married to TREVOR, old Boston, old money. Mother of three including BETSY, age 18.

FAWN LASSITER, 33, the family maverick—Bohemian, beautiful and aspiring opera star.

ROSAMOND LASSITER, 29, the family misfit, the "plain" Lassiter sister, who lives at home.

ROBERT LASSITER, 26, the only son; lost an arm while fighting in France during WWI.

DOWNSTAIRS

ARTHUR HACKER, 40, the English born butler who entered into the service of the Lassiter family in 1909. In 1915 he joined the British Army. Four years later, after seeing frontline action, he returned to the Lassiters and to his wife.

EMMELINE HACKER, 35, the Lassiter housekeeper in charge of the maids. She is hardworking, generous and profoundly Irish. She and Arthur, her husband, have their own suite in the Lassiter home.

BRIAN MALLORY, 26, the bright, ambitious bachelor nephew of Mrs. Hacker.

TERENCE O'HARA, 35, Hacker's assistant, pupil and disciple.

HARRY EMMET, 35, the family chauffeur who does "special" jobs for Benjamin Lassiter.

MARILYN GARDINER, 29, the distant, unmarried live-in secretary-companion to Mary Lassiter.

WILLIAM PIPER, 52, the family cook.

BEACON HILL

by Henry Clement

POPULAR LIBRARY • NEW YORK

POPULAR LIBRARY EDITION

This book is based on the television series, BEACON HILL, produced by The Robert Stigwood Organisation, Inc. Executive Producer: Beryl Vertue; Producer, Jacqueline Babbin. Material for this novel by Henry Clement was drawn largely from the teleplay by Sidney Carroll.

PRINTED IN THE UNITED STATES OF AMERICA

CHAPTER ONE:
LOUISBURG SQUARE: 1920

There is no disputing whatever the fact that, if you live in proper Boston, Beacon Hill is the proper place to live. Its streets are quiet, lined with soberly graceful townhouses, many of them designed by the great Charles Bulfinch himself. Over many of the doorways with their delicate fan lights, some of the glass panes are, indeed, the original ones, as centuries old as the houses themselves, and have turned a faint violet color with age.

Residents of Beacon Hill have, of course, an excellent view of the Charles River and of the bright golden dome of the State House, also a work of Bulfinch. It is only a short walk to the Common and to the Public Gardens with its swan boats and charming little bridge. At a convenient but discreet distance lies downtown Boston, with its stores and hotels and theaters. Behind the Hill, tactfully ignored by those who dwell on it, festers Scollay Square, with its seamy hotels, burlesque houses, cheap bars and the sordid establishments patronized by seamen and those who consort with them.

Beacon Hill, however, holds itself aloof from anything to do with commerce or the flesh. It has, since its very inception, been the stronghold of Brahmin Boston—noted for high thinking, plain living and Puritan respectability. Its inhabitants consider themselves "representative people," most of them living on the income of income. Beacon Hill's concept of original sin is dipping into capital.

It is also a matter of indisputable fact that, of all the addresses on Beacon Hill, the most desirable to have engraved in one's writing paper is "Number such-and-such, Louisburg Square," whose name commemorates a victory over the French in Canada by colonial Bostonians.

If you walk up Pinckney Street from the River you will, in a matter of minutes, come upon Louisburg Square, with its iron pickets, each topped with a molded spearhead, enclosing a grassy garden. In the center of the garden is a statue on a pedestal. It is the statue of an ancient worthy, his right hand tucked into the folds of his toga at his breast. Appropriately enough for the city known as the Athens of America, the statue represents Aristides, the Athenian statesman and general, known as "The Just."

All around Louisburg Square rise the largest and most imposing houses of Beacon Hill. Most of them are constructed of brick or redstone with contrasting trimming. The window frames are painted a creamy white. Now and then a curious passerby can catch a glimpse of a graceful Hepplewhite table with a Lowestoft bowl set on it, standing between carefully gathered damask draperies. The brass doorknobs and knockers are always highly polished, the dark green yews carefully clipped, the sidewalks swept twice daily. Voices are never raised in Louisburg Square. Even the private automobiles and the delivery trucks of the best Boston commercial establishments which make their way over the cobblestones that pave the Square, make their way with suitable quietness.

As for those cobblestones themselves, it is not recorded

who it was that remarked, "Those aren't cobblestones. Those are Irish heads."

Whoever it was, it was certainly someone of Hibernian descent, someone who had suffered at first hand from the attitude of Boston's Narrowbacks to the hungry wave of immigrants from the Emerald Isle.

For the Irish have never been masters on Beacon Hill. It is only in the servants' quarters that they were ever received with anything approximating a welcome. It was from their cramped rooms that they learned how the great houses of the Protestant gentry were run, how meals were served, how inherited old furniture was waxed and dusted. Watching everything around them carefully, they saw how the houses of the established rich were furnished, how their masters dressed and how they behaved and spoke. They learned quickly. After the second generation they were ready to copy their employers and, in a few instances, to edge them out and take their place.

The house which belonged to Benjamin Lassiter was one of the largest dwellings on Louisburg Square. It was even more immense than it appeared from its façade. Built of the customary redstone, like its neighbors, it had a pretentious heavy doorway above a wide stone stoop.

Perhaps the most interesting thing about the Lassiter house, insofar as the other residents of Louisburg Square were concerned, was the fact that not only did it not belong to its original owners, but that it represented "new money." More than that, it belonged to a family whose antecedents had arrived in Boston on one of those crowded immigrant boats which brought the Irish to its shores.

And it is behind the massive door of the Lassiter house that our story begins.

It begins on a January morning in the year 1920.

CHAPTER TWO:
THE NEW MAIDS

Appropriately enough, our story also begins below stairs, in the kitchen.

It was a vast room, replete with all the latest appliances of the time. The walls were covered with shining white tiles. Above the long wooden work table stretched a heavy iron rack from which hung a battery of shining pots and molds and metal implements. Behind it stood the black behemoth of a coal stove. At the far end, near the entrance to the stairway which led up to the dining room, the walls were lined with massive glass-enclosed cupboards, on the shelves of which were arrayed glistening services of china and Waterford crystal.

Mrs. Emmeline Hacker stood in the middle of the kitchen in her long black dress, a wide collar of starched lace at her throat and wide cuffs of matching lace at the edges of her long sleeves. Her bearing was stately and commanding. She was addressing two fresh-faced Irish girls who stood before her, attired in the standard Boston maid's uniform of black dress with white collar and cuffs. They fidgeted nervously under her cold inspecting glance. Behind Mrs. Hacker, silently watching, stood Eleanor

Murphy, in her frilled apron and ruffled cap. Now the chief parlor maid, although only in her twenties, Eleanor eyed the new girls critically. It was not so many years since she too had undergone Mrs. Hacker's first and harshly appraising review.

Emmeline Hacker was the Lassiters' housekeeper, in charge of the three maids. Stately and handsome, she was Irish and proud of it. Now she addressed the two new girls as though she were a headmistress or an army N.C.O. Stern-faced, she cast her eyes over them, not missing a single detail of their appearance.

"You will not speak unless spoke to," she told them. There was a strong brogue still in her voice. It seemed to lend to it even more of a sergeant-major's authority. "When you speak," she went on, "come to the point. Don't fiddle-faddle. Mr. and Mrs. Lassiter are good people and decent people if you know your place and do your job properly."

Kate and Maureen stared solemnly at her and nodded.

"You're green as grass and fresh off the boat," Mrs. Hacker went on severely, "and you hardly know your way around a civilized place as yet, but in time—" She broke off suddenly and stared at Maureen. It was a pointed stare.

Maureen was scratching herself.

"When," Mrs. Hacker inquired significantly, "did you take your bath, Maureen?"

In a burst of brogue as thick as a pat of Irish butter, Maureen retorted, "I'm not dirty, Aunt Em. It's the starch."

Mrs. Hacker pressed her lips into a thin line of reproof.

"In this house, when you talk to me, I am not your aunt!" she reminded the girl. "I am Mrs. Hacker. Why the devil can't you remember that?"

Maureen's cheeks flushed with quick color.

"I'm sorry," she said contritely. "I'll remember."

Mrs. Hacker tapped her pointed black shoe on the tile floor and waited.

"I'll remember, *Mrs. Hacker,*" Maureen amended, her cheeks flaming.

Mrs. Hacker's shoe ceased its tapping. She seemed, for the moment, appeased.

"You're me nieces, granted," she told the girls, "but let's not advertise the fact. It'll be all over Boston that I'm handing out paying jobs to every greenhorn who steps off the boat just because she's related to me Mick relatives back home." She turned abruptly to Kate, who seemed more concerned at the moment with whether her cap was set properly on her head than with what her aunt was saying.

"Katie," Mrs. Hacker demanded, "do you understand what I'm telling the two of youse?"

Katie sprang to attention.

"Yes, Aunt Em," she said.

Eleanor stepped forward.

"Ah," said Mrs. Hacker, "you take them in hand now, Eleanor. I give up. See if you can make silk purses out of them. I have a lot on my mind today. I can't spend all my blessed time educating the ignorant."

"I'll do my best, Mrs. Hacker," Eleanor said. "Come along, Maureen and Kate. I'll show you what's to be done upstairs."

The inspection of the new maids was over.

CHAPTER THREE:
IN THE CELLAR

While Mrs. Hacker was terminating her interview with the new maids, her husband, Arthur Hacker, was making his way down the cellar stairs with Terence O'Hara at his heels.

Hacker was the Lassiters' butler. He was a Londoner, born and bred in the shadow of Tower Bridge. He was a short man, but his way of standing made him seem considerably taller than he was. Prematurely gray, his carefully brushed hair rose above a furrowed forehead. He had been with the Lassiter family ever since he had come to the United States in 1909, at the age of twenty-nine. In 1915 he left to join the British army. He had spent two years in the trenches, in France, serving with the Rifle Brigade. Badly wounded by shrapnel, he had spent a year recovering in army hospitals. Early in 1919 he returned to the Lassiters and to his wife.

Hacker was an excellent butler. He took tremendous pride in what he called "the profession." His tone was always slightly professional, his face always dead sober, even when he was having his little joke. His professorial air was even more pronounced because of his habitually slow speech: Hacker, very proud of his London heritage, took particular pains to observe every grammatical nicety.

Terence O'Hara had a long solemn face with hollow eyesockets and a slack mouth. He was Hacker's assistant, pupil and disciple. When he had time, he also served as valet to the Lassiter men: Benjamin, the head of the family, and to his son, Robert. He took his duties very seriously. In fact, O'Hara took everything seriously, constantly mulling over what was told to him.

Hacker paused on the cellar stairs.

"I suppose you must often stop to wonder, Mr. O'Hara," he remarked, "how it could come about that a prototypical Englishman like myself could marry a lass like Mrs. Hacker?"

O'Hara's mouth fell open.

"What?" He reflected solemnly. "Oh, no, sir," he declared. "I never wonder that."

Hacker descended to the cellar floor. They moved forward into the confines of the basement before he spoke again.

"The reason is very simple, Mr. O'Hara," he said portentously. "Mrs. Hacker happens to be immensely wealthy."

O'Hara stared at Hacker in astonishment.

"She is?"

"Heiress to untold millions," proclaimed Mr. Hacker.

"Why, Mr. Hacker," O'Hara gasped. "You never . . ." Then a light suddenly dawned on O'Hara's mental horizon. "Ahh," he exclaimed, "you're having your little joke, Mr. Hacker! I'm stupid enough to bite every time."

Hacker, chuckling drily, made an abrupt turn, with an abashed O'Hara still at his heels. They now emerged into a deep cool canyon lined with great walls of wine bottles.

Hacker waved his hand at the prospect.

"Take a good look, Mr. O'Hara," he proclaimed. "Take

a deep breath, then a good look. At midnight, Friday, all this becomes illegal."

The two men stared at Benjamin Lassiter's well-stocked cellar.

The Eighteenth Amendment to the Constitution of the United States of America, which said of alcoholic beverages that "the manufacture, sale, or transportation thereof into, or the exportation thereof from the U.S. and all territories subject to the jurisdiction thereof for beverage purposes" was prohibited, had been approved by the necessary thirty-six states on January 16, 1919. The Volstead Act was passed immediately afterward to enforce the Prohibition Amendment. It defined an intoxicating beverage as one which contained one half of one percent alcohol. In addition, it imposed severe penalties for violations of the Act.

Millions of well-meaning people believed that the ratification of the Eighteenth Amendment would put a miraculous end to the liquor problem. The sale of intoxicants would at once cease, and with that cessation, poverty and crime would largely disappear.

But millions of other Americans had an entirely different attitude toward alcoholic beverages. They had been brought up in households where beer or wine was served with the family meal.

And now, on the eve of that strange era on which the Eighteenth Amendment and the Volstead Act were to leave their wild and indelible mark, Hacker and O'Hara surveyed the contents of the cellar.

"But he can go on keeping it, can't he?" O'Hara inquired. "It's his own personal property."

"It is liquor, Mr. O'Hara," Hacker replied. *"Liquor!"* He repeated the word emphatically. "At midnight, on Friday, it becomes an unlawful possession. You can't sell it. You can't drink it. You can't own it. I'm not quite sure even if you can *talk* about it. I find the new law not quite explicit on that point. However—" He stopped to examine the nearest row of bottles. "However," he continued, "the question before the house at the moment is: which of these golden bottles, so soon to be branded bootleg, do we serve the master for his homecoming?"

The two men were now involved in a game which they both obviously enjoyed to the hilt.

"A Pinot Noir, Mr. Hacker?" O'Hara suggested cautiously. "One of the Tissots? Say the year '12 or '11?"

Hacker shook his head.

"Too exotic, Mr. O'Hara," he commented. "You go too, too far . . ."

Terence O'Hara soberly eyed his mentor.

"Then I would say, perhaps . . ." he began.

From overhead, the voice of Mrs. Hacker cut through the distance between them and the kitchen like a clarion call to arms.

"Mr. Hacker!"

"My dear?" Mr. Hacker called back, mildly.

"They're here!"

Mr. Hacker regretfully surveyed the arrayed bottles.

"Well, Mr. O'Hara," he remarked, "all this will have to wait for a later moment of decision. Right now, Mr. O'Hara, duty calls!"

Majestically performing an about-face, Mr. Hacker proceeded up the stairs, O'Hara solemnly following a pace behind him.

CHAPTER FOUR: HOMECOMING

At the curb outside the house a long black Packard limousine was being emptied of its passengers.

Benjamin Lassiter had already stepped out of the car. Now he stood planted on the pavement, contemplating his house. He eyed it with a mixture of satisfaction and relief: satisfaction at having attained it, and relief at having returned to it after an absence. The house on Louisburg Square meant a great deal to Ben Lassiter, more than he would ever admit, even to himself. He was a totally self-made man, and what he had made, he had made the hard way, butting himself upward. He had made a lot of money by the time he was thirty. Now, in his middle sixties, he was established in every way he wished to be. Tough and smart, he was ruthlessly professional in his calling, and his calling was politics. He was the gray eminence in Boston's City Hall, and that made him not only a power throughout Massachusetts, but also in the national party. In addition to his own fortune, he had married a lot of money. His wife, Mary, was the daughter of an Irish brickmaker who became a building contractor. When he died, the old man left his daughter two million dollars.

Ben Lassiter had compounded his own money and his wife's into a more-than-respectable fortune. Now, with the profits which the war had brought him, he was ready for the really big money. He was prepared to join the small clique of the very rich, a prospect which to him was no less agreeable than that of his impressive Louisburg Square property.

In addition to all this, Ben Lassiter prided himself on being a good father and a good husband. As to his church, he was prepared to be religious when it served his purposes. He dressed with quiet, sober immaculateness. Flash was a thing which Ben Lassiter might appreciate in others, but he did not care for it much when it came to his own person. "A gentleman," he liked to say, "is never more than correct in his dress and his behavior—and," he would add, with a quiet twinkle, "never less." He was getting portly now, but Ben Lassiter still moved with a youthful spring. And his face, below his carefully groomed head of thinning white hair, was fully fleshed and ruddy.

Ben Lassiter's associate, Marvin Malloy, an unimpressive man in his fifties, stood at his side, waiting for a word from the great man. Lassiter, however, was too busy with his own thoughts to address any remarks to him. He merely stood there, regarding the house and smiling with pleasure at the sight of it.

It was now Mary Lassiter's turn to emerge from the limousine. A tall woman, wrapped in a thick chinchilla stole and wearing a vast broad-bimmed hat trimmed with a single aigrette, she carried a slender ebony cane. Harry Emmet, the family chauffeur, in livery and high laced boots, held the door of the Packard, while Marilyn Gardiner, Mary Lassiter's secretary and companion, helped her out.

"Oh, Marilyn," Mary Lassiter exclaimed, "it's good to

be back." She drew a deep breath. "I even love the smell of Boston!"

At that moment a taxicab pulled up to the curb behind the limousine. It was loaded inside and out with suitcases.

The moment it stopped, Rosamond Lassiter popped out of the rear door. Rosamond was the youngest of the four Lassiter daughters. Boston charitably referred to her as "the plain Lassiter girl." And she was, to tell the truth, rather plain, with a small peaked face, a thin-lipped, slightly too wide mouth and mousy hair, partially concealed now by a hat which on another woman might have been becoming but which on her merely appeared fussy and frumpish. She wore a too-long sealskin coat which she had never bothered to have shortened.

Now she turned officiously to the cabdriver. "First take the baggage off the top, then help get the stuff inside," she ordered, in her high, spinsterish voice. "Emmet!" she called. "Will you give this man a hand? And when you pay him, give him a good tip. He's a very good driver." She swung back to the driver. "What's your name?" she demanded.

"Carmody, Miss," he said, touching the peak of his cap. "Arthur Carmody."

"Arthur Carmody," she repeated quickly. "Greater Boston Cab Company. I'll remember that, make no mistake."

By now there was a mild turmoil on the pavement in front of the house. Everyone was talking at once and cases were being moved into the house. Then the front door opened and O'Hara emerged.

He came running down the steps.

"O'Hara," Rosamond called, "will you come over here and help this man with the luggage?"

"Right away, Miss Rosamond," he replied. But instead of helping with the luggage he saluted Ben Lassiter with eager deference.

"Welcome home, Mr. Lassiter!" he said.

Lassiter smiled at him.

"Thanks, O'Hara," he said.

With a swelling chest, O'Hara advanced to Mrs. Lassiter. He carefully took her arm.

"Welcome home, Mrs. Lassiter," he told her in a low earnest voice.

"O'Hara!" Rosamond cried from the taxi. "Did you hear me ask—"

"Rosamond," her mother called out sharply. "Keep your voice down. It's me first, then the baggage!"

"I was only suggesting . . ." Rosamond expostulated. Her voice died away as another car, chauffeur-driven, pulled up behind the others.

Before its chauffeur had time enough to step out of the car and open the door for its occupant, the rear door burst open and Betsy Bullock came tearing along the sidewalk to throw herself into her grandfather's arms.

"Hi, Grandpa!" she exclaimed. "Welcome home!"

A grin of delight passed across Ben Lassiter's face. "Why, hello, darlin'!" he replied, putting on a bit of brogue as he hugged the child to him. It was an old game between them. Then he pushed her a few inches away from him and regarded her. She had a pert little face, framed with light hair, and a trim figure. Benjamin Lassiter had always enjoyed the sight of pretty young girls, and looking at his eighteen-year-old granddaughter, the oldest child of his second daughter Emily, gave him unconcealed pleasure.

And now Emily herself emerged in stately fashion from the limousine. She was, as always, splendidly turned out. Her tall hat, in the height of fashion, and her vast muff both served to emphasize her slender figure. At forty, she was still a beauty, although if one looked closely the caustic lines of her face were to be seen beneath its layer of powder and languor. Her spectacular appearance, so different from that of the usual run of drably dressed Boston matrons, compelled Arthur Carmody to stop unloading the suitcases for a moment and goggle openly at her.

Emily Bullock crossed the pavement, conscious of the effect she was creating, and went over to kiss her mother on the cheek.

"Mother, did you have a nice time?" Emily asked in her flat North Shore drawl.

"Hello, dear," Mary Lassiter replied. "Did I have a nice time?" She made a wry face. "I don't know."

Then Betsy ran over to her.

"Grandma!" she cried, embracing her.

"Hello, my love," Mary Lassiter said. She frowned. "Only *one* grandchild greets me on this auspicious occasion?" She glanced around, as though looking for the others.

Emily remarked in a faintly annoyed tone, "I *couldn't* take the others out of school."

"Why not?" Mary Lassiter said sharply. She turned to Rosamond. "Rosamond," she demanded, "where are the trunks?"

"They're coming in the truck, Mother!" Rosamond answered with a touch of exasperation in her voice. "You can't get trunks into a taxicab, you know!"

"Why can't you?" Mary Lassiter wanted to know.

Rosamond's reply, if she bothered to make one, was lost in the general babble. Emily was explaining to her mother why her husband, Trevor Bullock, couldn't make it. Benjamin Lassiter and Betsy had already started up the steps, accompanied by the mute and deferential Malloy. Rosamond remained behind supervising fussily, while Carmody fumbled with the baggage.

O'Hara, his face grave with the responsibility, was trying to urge Mary Lassiter up the steps.

Mrs. Lassiter, however, lingered to demand of Emily, "Where's Maude? And where's that husband and those children of hers? And what about Fawn? My God, you'd think that if they couldn't come down to meet the boat they could at least meet us here!"

"But they're coming, Mother," Emily assured her.

"Do you mean to say that Maude couldn't manage to come down to the boat to meet her parents?" Mary Lassiter persisted, her voice beginning to rise imperiously. "And as for Fawn. . . !"

"Miss Gardiner," Rosamond called out. "Are you sure that you have the tickets for the steamer trunks? I didn't—"

"Oh, yes! I'm positive," Miss Gardiner cried. "They ought to be arriving any moment now. The man at the pier promised me—"

Eventually, O'Hara managed to coax Mrs. Lassiter up the steps. She went slowly, assisted by her cane. Emily Bullock stalked after her mother, her mouth set in annoyance at her sisters who had failed to come when expected and had left her to bear the brunt of their mother's disappointment.

The last to go through the massive front door of the house on Louisburg Square, after all the suitcases had finally been unloaded from the taxicab, were Rosamond, somewhat flustered from all the activity, and Miss Gardiner, who, as always, did her best to remain unobtrusive. Miss Gardiner, at least, knew her place.

The Lassiters had come home to Beacon Hill.

CHAPTER FIVE: THE HENCHMEN IN THE HALL

They were already there, waiting for Ben Lassiter in the vast airy hall.

John Broderick, a big man with a walrus moustache and pepper-and-salt hair brushed across his forehead, was ensconced in an elaborately carved throne-chair. He leaned his head back against the dark tapestry upholstery and chomped on a dead cigar. He held his derby hat in his lap and eyed with shrewd speculation the great curving staircase and the Greek Revival pilasters. His feet, in highly shined black shoes encased in pearl-gray spats, were set solidly on the marble floor. His heavy gold watch chain gleamed against the well-cut English serge of his double-breasted vest.

John Broderick, Boston's mayor, was an important man, and he knew it. He also knew that Ben Lassiter had a considerable role to play in his own importance.

Beside Broderick stood an insignificant, clerkish type, pale of complexion and blinking mole-like from behind steel-rimmed eyeglasses. Alvin Morse was the kind of man who is continually awed by strange surroundings. It was not the first time he had made an appearance in Lassiter's house, but he never failed to reveal, with a slight gape of his dry mouth and a faintly dazed expression in his pale eyes, the fact that he was not only impressed by the house itself but also was aware of the privilege conferred upon him by being there.

On the other side of the room Mrs. Hacker stood, her hands folded in front of her, facing the front door. Eleanor and Kate and Maureen were lined up at attention behind her. None of them dared twitch at their aprons or so much as raise a hand to adjust a frilled cap. They knew only too well that while Mrs. Hacker's gaze was concentrated on the front door she still would not fail to miss any inadvertent move they made.

Hacker, on duty at the front door itself, ran his fingers across the knot of his tie, making sure that it set properly against the stiff wing tips of his starched collar. He peered through the muslin stretched across the plate glass of the door. His gloved hand hovered over the knob.

Then he turned to Mrs. Hacker and gave her a quick nod.

They were coming up the steps at last!

Now Hacker pounced on the knob and swung the door open.

Benjamin Lassiter stepped across his threshold with his granddaughter Betsy on his arm and Molloy, bursting with loyalty and self-importance, close on their heels.

Before anyone else could speak, John Broderick had jumped to his feet. He advanced with his right hand outstretched and a broad smile of greeting on his ruddy face.

"Ben!" he bellowed. "How are you?"

"Hello, John," said Lassiter, briskly, ignoring his hand.

Broderick cleared his throat.

"Sorry we couldn't make it to meet you at the boat," he said.

"Well, it took us longer than we thought it would to get

through Customs," Lassiter informed him drily. He turned to Hacker. "Hello, Hacker," he said with a smile.

"Welcome home, Mr. Lassiter," Hacker said gravely.

"Customs!" exclaimed Broderick.

Lassiter ignored him. He flashed a cordial smile at Morse.

"Hello, Alvin," he said.

Morse beamed. He appreciated being noticed. "Nice to see you, Mr. Lassiter," he said.

Broderick chewed his moustache. "You went through Customs?" he bellowed, blustering. "Why the hell didn't you let me know? You didn't have to go through Customs!"

"*You* should have thought of that," Lassiter replied, striding past him to greet the housekeeper. "Hello, Mrs. Hacker," he said. "How's the home team?"

"Fine, thank you, sir," she replied. "Welcome home."

Broderick was at Lassiter's elbow.

"Ben," he boomed contritely, "it just never occurred to me." He twiddled the brim of his hat. "Just dumb, I guess," he said.

Lassiter continued to ignore him.

Broderick looked around in embarrassment. He caught Malloy's eye. "Hello, Malloy," he said.

"Hello, your Honor," Malloy replied, briefly.

Lassiter squinted toward the new parlormaids.

"And what have we here?" he asked Mrs. Hacker.

"Mr. Lassiter," she began, "I would like—"

He cut her off with a wave of his hand. "Later, Mrs. Hacker. Later." He turned to Betsy. "Will I see you tonight?" he asked her. "Are you coming to dinner?"

"I've got a date tonight, Grandpa," she told him.

He stared at her. Then he grinned. "By God, you are that age, are you? Leave you alone for six weeks, and what happens?"

She grinned back at him. "Nothing special happens, Grandpa!" she said.

"You grow up!"

"I'm eighteen," she reminded him, with a flash of her dimples.

He shook his head, as though in utter wonderment.

"You were twelve the day before yesterday!" he said. He shrugged. Then he turned to Broderick. "Come on, Mr. Mayor," he said.

He strode across the hall toward the door which led to his study. Broderick, Malloy and Morse followed him. Once the men had vanished into the room, the door closed firmly behind them.

CHAPTER SIX: A GATHERING OF THE FAMILY

At the moment when Benjamin Lassiter's study door closed on him and his political cronies, Mary Lassiter made her slow and stately entrance into the house, accompanied by her daughter Emily Bullock and Marilyn Gardiner. Rosamond had come as far as the front door and then dashed out into the street again to make sure that Emmet was seeing properly to the luggage.

"Welcome home, Mrs. Lassiter," Hacker said.

Mrs. Hacker hurried forward to relieve her of the sheaf of red roses bound with a huge knot of satin ribbon that she carried.

"Welcome home, Mrs. Lassiter," she said with a smile.

"Thank you, thank you!" Mary Lassiter exclaimed. She stood there, perfectly still for a moment, resting her weight on her slender ebony cane and glancing around her, as though infinitely relieved to be home at last. The cold winter sunlight was streaming down from the circular window of the staircase. She moved a step or two forward into it. Her long, fine-boned face, under the elegant black hat with its soaring plume, suddenly appeared ashen and tired, but she nonetheless managed a warm smile.

Marilyn Gardiner glanced at her with a trace of concern, ready to move forward and take her arm, but Mary Lassiter shook her head.

"I'm quite all right, Marilyn," she said.

Hacker cleared his throat.

"Welcome home, Miss Gardiner," he said. He liked her, and there was more than professional politeness in his greeting. Marilyn Gardiner wasn't exactly a girl anymore, she was close to thirty if a day, but she still had a soft, mousy prettiness which appealed to him. Furthermore, she was careful never to make demands on the staff. After all, she was practically one of them. He eyed her, small and unobstrusive in her modest hat and last year's cloak, wondering if she had enjoyed the trip.

"Thank you, Mr. Hacker," Marilyn said, warmly.

There was a girl for you, Hacker thought. She might be mousy and missish, but she knew how to smile and her eyes had a quiet twinkle in them.

Benjamin Lassiter suddenly stuck his head out of the study door.

"Where's Rob?" he demanded.

"Mr. Robert," Hacker informed him, "is expected at any moment."

A frown of impatience appeared on Mr. Lassiter's forehead. Then he nodded. "Send him in as soon as he gets here," he ordered. Then he jerked his chin in the direction of Emily. "Then I want to see Miss Emily—"

"Father," Emily broke in, "I don't really think I can stick around all morning."

Benjamin Lassiter briefly considered his daughter's reply. He left it unanswered. "Then Miss Maude," he went on, "if she ever gets here. Then Miss Fawn, ditto. In that order."

"Yes, Mr. Lassiter," Hacker said. "I'll see to it."

Lassiter withdrew once more into the study, closing the door behind him.

Hacker and Miss Gardiner exchanged a look.

"Run along with Hacker, Miss Gardiner," Mary Lassiter told her. "I'm sure you have a great many things to go over together. I'll see you later."

Marilyn rummaged in her capacious handbag. "I have your lists right here, Mrs. Lassiter. Hacker, just give me a minute to get rid of my hat and I'll be with you."

Hacker sedately followed her out.

Betsy Bullock went up to her grandmother.

"Grandma," she said. "I've got to go."

"Why?" Mary Lassiter asked sharply.

Betsy made a face. "I've got to study. Exams tomorrow," she answered quickly. She reached up and kissed her grandmother's cheek. "I'll come by as soon as I can," she promised.

"I hope that'll be sometime before you reach middle age," Mrs. Lassiter remarked.

"Oh, Grandma!" Betsy cried. "Why do you always have to say things like that?"

"Because they're true. That's why."

Betsy kissed her again. She waved her hand at Emily. " 'Bye, Mama!" she called. And then she flew out of the house.

Emily Bullock's eyes narrowed and her lips twitched faintly.

"That child is getting to be such a liar," she began. "She—"

Her mother cut her off pointedly. Turning to the parlormaid, she said, "Hello, Eleanor."

Eleanor bobbed.

"Welcome home, I'm sure, Mrs. Lassiter," she said.

Mary Lassiter's glance traveled then to the two new girls waiting nervously beside Eleanor.

"Wel-l-l-l, Mrs. Hacker!" she said.

Mrs. Hacker moved a step forward.

"Mrs. Lassiter," she said, "I would like to introduce

two young ladies we took on while you were abroad. This is Kate Mehaffey and this is Maureen Mehaffey. Cousins, they are." She flashed the girls a quick signal with her eyes. They curtsied, not too clumsily.

Just then Rosamond's voice could be heard from the front stairs.

"Emmet, will you see to the rest of the luggage when the truck comes?"

Mary Lassiter regarded the two new girls, taking in every detail of their fresh country faces under their newly starched caps, their raw hands, their carefully washed hair.

"When did you girls get off the boat?" she asked.

Mrs. Hacker hastily answered for them.

"They arrived two weeks ago, Mrs. Lassiter," she said.

Rosamond finally burst through the front door.

"Oh," she exclaimed. "You've met the girls, Mother."

"Yes," Mrs. Lassiter said.

"This is Katie, and this is Maureen," Rosamond went on in a rush. "I hope you've told Mrs. Lassiter that you're going to night school?"

"What for?" Mary Lassiter asked. "To learn English?"

Rosamond heaved a heavy sigh.

"Oh, Mother—"

"They've got to learn the Constitution and all that," Mrs. Hacker hastened to explain, "if they're going to become citizens."

"The Constitution and all that," Mary Lassiter repeated thoughtfully. A faint twinkle appeared in her light blue eyes. "When you learn it, girls," she said, "you'll have to teach it to me."

Eleanor repressed a smile. Kate and Maureen stared at the floor and tried not to giggle.

Benjamin Lassiter once again stuck his head out of the door of the study.

"Rob here yet?"

"Not yet, sir," Mrs. Hacker answered.

"As soon as he comes in—" he began.

"Yes, sir." Mrs. Hacker assured him. As he was about to withdraw his head once more, Mrs. Hacker said sharply, "Now then, Maureen!" She nodded in Mrs. Lassiter's direction. "Go ahead and say what I told you to say."

Benjamin Lassiter lingered curiously in the doorway to watch what was going on.

Maureen took a single uncertain step forward.

"Good afternoon, Madam," she managed to articulate in the general direction of Mrs. Lassiter.

"Now the other one?" Mary Lassiter inquired.

Mrs. Hacker yanked sharply at Kate's apron.

"Go on!" she said. "Prove *you've* got a tongue in your head."

"Afternoon, mum," Kate managed to say.

"Brilliant," remarked Mrs. Hacker.

"Say it, girls," Mrs. Lassiter told them. "Don't hum it."

"Now," Mrs. Hacker ordered the new recruits, "follow me." She started to lead them out to the kitchen.

Benjamin Lassiter stepped forward and halted the small procession before it got started.

"Just a minute," he called.

He advanced and squinted carefully at the girls.

"County Limerick, Mrs. Hacker?" he demanded.

"Where else, then?" came the prompt reply.

"Relations of yours?"

"Well, sir, as a matter of fact," Mrs. Hacker began, fingering the gold cross at her throat, "they—"

He nodded resignedly. "More nieces," he said. "I know, Mrs. Hacker."

He vanished into the study again, the door silently closing after him. Mrs. Hacker nodded briefly and significantly at the girls and marched them out to the kitchen. Emily Bullock was left alone with her mother.

"Now then," demanded Mary Lassiter, "why couldn't you come to the boat?"

Emily raised her hands to adjust her towering hat with its fall of jet black coq feathers. "Really, Mother—" she began.

The doorbell rang, cutting her off, rather to her relief.

O'Hara appeared and crossed the hall to the vestibule and opened the door.

Maude, the oldest of the Lassiter daughters, swept in with her husband, Richard Palmer. Maude Palmer was a tall woman in her late thirties, fine-boned like her mother. In time she might even acquire some of Mary Lassiter's style. Still, like her sister Emily, she was a great beauty and carried herself with the self-possession of a woman accusomed to the appreciation and admiration of the world at large. She was well turned out. Her long cloak was simple and well cut, her tri-cornered hat unadorned except for a trimming of soutache braid at the corners. The long pointed shoes she had on emphasized her slender ankles. She did not create the stunning impression of Emily, with her rather theatrical and dashing way of dressing, but it was Maude's image which lasted longer in the memory. If Emily Bullock possessed all the dazzling surface brilliance of a portrait by Boldini, then her elder sister was a John Singer Sargent at his best.

Richard Palmer was a few years older than Maude. Tall, slender, sandy-haired and athletic, his pale myopic eyes shielded with spectacles, he was pleasant and good-natured, if somewhat dull. Still, the Lassiters had been pleased with the match, and even more pleased with the four grandchildren which the Palmers had dutifully produced.

Maude ran forward and embraced her mother.

"Welcome home, Mama!" she cried.

Mary Lassiter held Maude close for an instant. Then she drew back. "Where are the children?" she asked.

"In school, Mama. I didn't think you'd want me to—"

Over Maude's shoulder, Mary held out her hand to her son-in-law.

"Welcome home," he told her. "We've missed you!" he exclaimed, blinking earnestly.

Marilyn Gardiner quietly reappeared, in her shirtwaist and skirt, on her way upstairs. She flashed a glance of discreet concern at Mrs. Lassiter.

Mary Lassiter caught her eye, abruptly pushed Maude from her arms, and drew a handkerchief from her chinchilla muff. She sniffed, wiped the corner of an eye and extended her hand to Marilyn.

"I'm beginning to realize that I'm home," she said. "Which means that I may cry. Miss Gardiner, take me upstairs and make me wash my face." She gave the others a wan smile. "I'll see you all," she said, "in a little while."

Marilyn Gardiner helped her proceed slowly up the stairs.

There was a long silence in the hall after they had gone.

The two beautiful Lassiter sisters eyed one another with a look of cold appraisal.

Richard Palmer tactfully broke the silence.

"How are you, Em?" he said cheerfully.

"Fine and dandy," she answered in a toneless voice. She turned to Maude. "Hello," she said.

"Hello," Maude replied.

"Where's Trev?" Richard asked.

"Busy," Emily said in the same toneless manner.

There was another moment of cool silence.

It was broken this time by the sudden opening of the study door. Benjamin Lassiter stuck his head out.

"Where's—" he shouted.

Then he saw Maude.

"Ah!" he cried.

He bounded out, surprisingly light on his feet for his

age and growing portliness. He kissed Maude affectionately. Then he stood back and beamed at her.

"I'm sorry we couldn't get to the boat, Father," she told him. "What happened was—"

He held up a hand to halt her explanations. "That's okay. It's okay." He went over to Richard Palmer. "How are you, Richard?"

The two men shook hands.

"Oh, fine!" Palmer said. "Just fine!"

"Do a lot of yachting in Florida?" Lassiter asked.

"Well—" Palmer began.

But before he could launch into a description of his sailing in Florida, Lassiter cut in. "Where are the kids?" he inquired, looking around for them.

"They go to school, Daddy!" Maude reminded him.

He looked slightly crestfallen.

"So they do," he murmured. His eyes absently traveled around the hall. "Fawn come yet?"

"Not yet," Emily put in pointedly.

"What about Rob?" he wanted to know. "Has Rob come?"

"*I* haven't seen him," Emily said.

Benjamin Lassiter cleared his throat. "Well," he said. "In that case—" He started for the study door. As he walked past Palmer he paused and looked into Palmer's bland face. "Or is the word 'boating'?" he suddenly asked.

"What?" Richard blinked. "Oh! Well," he said, "as a matter of fact, it all depends on—"

Lassiter waved his hands in the air. "Don't bother!" he said with a shake of his head. "I'll never get it straight."

He disappeared into his study.

Emily, Maude and Richard stood there, staring at the door.

Once again an awkward silence descended over them.

Finally Emily smiled and turned to her brother-in-law.

When she spoke her tone was mild, but there was no mistaking the sneer in her voice.

"He adores you, darling," she said.

"Shut your mouth, Emily," Maude flashed.

CHAPTER SEVEN: AFFAIRS OF STATE

Benjamin Lassiter's study, as it was called, was not a room habitually devoted to contemplation. To be sure, there were the rows of leather-bound classics which Goodspeed's had supplied to fill the shelves, but they had never been touched. If you opened one of the volumes, the gilt edgings would cause the pages to stick. The bindings themselves, however, made a handsome show.

It was a room heavily paneled in dark wood. Over the massive mantelpiece hung a murky portrait, vaguely of the Spanish School. There was a desk there, to be sure. Lassiter used it chiefly as a hedge between himself and any petitioners who came to see him. There were four or five heavy easy chairs set about on the rugs, some odd tables which could serve, if necessary, to hold a highball, and a small sideboard loaded with whisky and glasses.

Malloy was standing at the sideboard, solemnly spraying seltzer from a tall syphon into a glass. Eventually he handed it to Broderick, who sat facing Benjamin Lassiter and listening with rapt attention to what Lassiter was saying. He still held his dead cigar between his teeth.

Morse, clutching his briefcase, kept in the background. No one could ever accuse him of not knowing his place.

Broderick leaned forward.

"But, Ben," he put in, "Christy says—"

Lassiter slapped the top of his desk. "I don't give a damn what Christy has to say. If the Third District is a hundred and sixty registrations short, tell Christy to make it good, or he'll find himself back where he started, selling Rotherham's popcorn at Revere Beach!"

Broderick shook his head reproachfully.

"Ben," he said. "One hundred and sixty stinkin' votes!"

"Him and that fat brother of his," Lassiter snapped back, "that you put in that cushy job in Dedham!"

Broderick held up a plump conciliating hand.

"It may not be Christy's fault!" he pleaded.

"Then it's your fault, Mr. Mayor," Benjamin called out. "If your appointees can't keep the registrations in line, then let us examine your talent for filling the organization with nincompoops. All right. Now tell me about Friday night."

The Mayor took a long gulp of his drink, expelled a blast of air and leaned back more easily in his chair.

"Well, Ben," he said, "every hotel's been booked for months. Every cafe in town is gonna be loaded for the festivities with the steady customers—"

"Festivities?" Lassiter broke in.

"Sure, Ben. The town's going to go crazy! Friday night'll be the same as New Year's Eve. Why, they're already calling it the Second New Year's Eve."

Lassiter remarked thoughtfully, "It sounds more like the second coming of the flood."

Broderick emitted an appreciative guffaw. "Yeah!" he said. "Flood's the word for it. The intention of John Q. Public is to drink every hotel, every restaurant, every saloon and every cafe bone-dry before midnight rolls around."

"Well, they're not going to accomplish that," Lassiter told him matter-of-factly. "So what happens at twelve, John? Are you really going to close them up?"

The Mayor ruminated for a moment. "Well," he said at last, "I intended to ask you about that. The Governor's already voiced his sentiments."

"I can imagine what they are."

"Yeah. Well, Mr. Coolidge wants strict enforcement."

"Then give him strict enforcement."

"That's what I was hoping you'd say, Ben. Strict enforcement is what the Governor's going to get from the minute the Prohibition Law goes into effect. Every cop in the city of Boston is going to be on the job that night, whether he's regular day force or night force. At twelve o'clock midnight, right on the dot, not one damned minute after, we're going to close down every saloon in this town and we're going to confiscate every bottle of liquor they've got left on the premises." He paused and moved his cigar to the other side of his mouth. "What's your opinion?" he asked.

Lassiter considered. "What's the penalty if they're open after twelve?" he asked.

"Tough, Ben. Tough. A day in jail and a hundred-dollar fine," the Mayor told him.

"All right. And what about John Q. Public caught with liquor in his own house?" Lassiter wanted to know.

"Same thing. Day in jail, hundred bucks fine."

Lassiter leaned forward.

"Tell me this, John," he said. "Do you think that's going to stop it?"

John Broderick carefully removed the dead cigar from his mouth, examined it briefly and deposited it in an ashtray, as though laying it to rest in a crystal coffin.

"It'll stop it dead in its tracks," he said.

CHAPTER EIGHT: STEAK TARTARE

Downstairs in the kitchen, Hacker and O'Hara were scrutinizing the label on a bottle of wine.

"Are we sufficiently stocked with the '09 that we can use a bottle for luncheon?" Hacker asked.

O'Hara nodded. "I counted them this morning, Mr. Hacker," he said. "We have seventy-three bottles left. That should last till Friday."

"Friday!" Hacker exclaimed. "It's the fatal day. I keep forgetting."

William Piper, the cook, tall, black, his solid face gleaming with beads of perspiration and a napkin knotted around his thick neck, lumbered across the kitchen with a heavy tray loaded down with silver and glassware. He set it down in front of Hacker and waited silently for the butler's approval.

Hacker lifted the silver lid of a serving dish and sniffed at the food. His nose wrinkled with undisguised distaste. O'Hara peered at the dish over Hacker's shoulder.

"You insist on serving this?" he asked Piper.

Piper replaced the lid.

"It's steak tartare," he declared. "It's his favorite."

O'Hara looked grave.

"You don't approve of raw meat in a sandwich, Mr. Hacker?"

Hacker drew on his white mutton-cloth gloves.

"Given the choice," he pronounced, "I would choose capital punishment."

And, having expressed his opinion, he gripped the handles of the tray and marched out of the kitchen with it, leaving O'Hara and Piper to stare open-mouthed after him.

CHAPTER NINE: THE LAW OF THE LAND

In Benjamin Lassiter's study the delegation from City Hall was still discussing the Prohibition Act and its possible consequences. Or, rather, Mayor Broderick was holding forth to Lassiter, while Malloy and Morse sat in the background and listened.

"But what we are facing, I'm sure, and we'd better get ready for it, is a real estate crisis," Broderick announced.

Lassiter got up from behind his desk and leaned against the mantelpiece.

"How so, John?" he asked.

"Ben," Broderick pursued, "do you know how many saloons are going to be empty on Saturday morning? How many vacated premises there are going to be? Thousands!" He repeated the word ponderously. "Thousands! And who's going to move into those properties when they move out?"

"That's an easy one to answer," Ben said.

"Yeah? Answer it, then."

"I'll tell you. Candy stores, doughnut parlors, soft drink emporiums—and saloons."

Broderick gasped.

"Saloons?"

Lassiter went over and stood in front of the Mayor's chair. "John, you don't seriously think they're *all* going to go out of business?" he asked.

"Ben!" Broderick's voice rose. "Friday, midnight, it'll be against the law!"

"So's prostitution," Lassiter remarked mildly.

Broderick made a disapproving face. He did his best to disregard the distasteful word. "Six thousand police I've got to enforce Prohibition," he went on, "*and* the Watch and Ward Society, *and* the Internal Revenue Agents for the Boston District, *and* the Anti-Saloon League, *and* the Women's Christian Temperance Union, *and* the Allied Citizens of America, *and* one thousand blue-nosed pastors representing twenty-five religious denominations—and the will of the people! This is now the law of the land, Ben. Or it will be, on Saturday morning. And it was voted that way by the people of the United States." He pulled out a handkerchief from his breast pocket and mopped his forehead with it. "You think any saloonkeeper is going to try and stay in business in the face of all that?"

He was interrupted by a quiet knock on the door.

"Yes?" Lassiter called.

The door opened and Hacker entered the room carrying the tray.

"Ah!" Lassiter said. He rubbed his hands together. "Gentlemen," he said, "how about you, too? Will you have a bite with me?"

Broderick slowly got to his feet. Malloy and Morse were already standing.

"No thanks, Ben," the Mayor said.

Malloy held up his hands. "Not me," he exclaimed.

As for Morse, he inaudibly murmured something about its being too early in the day.

Hacker set the tray on a table. There was a bottle on it. Lassiter picked it up and consulted the label.

"Sarsaparilla, Mr. Mayor," he remarked.

Broderick let out a loud bray of laughter. Morse discreetly sniggered.

Then, without further ceremony, Lassiter sat down and picked up the sandwich. He smiled appreciatively and nodded at Hacker who was opening the whisky bottle.

"Steak tartare," he said. "My favorite!"

At that moment there was another knock on the door of the study. Hacker went and opened it.

The young man who stood framed in the doorway had an easy, attractive grin on his face. His dark hair was neatly slicked down over his skull. He had the regular good looks featured in the advertisements for Arrow collars. He was quietly dressed in a dark lounge suit, with a thick dark tie knotted neatly at the opening of his high starched collar. He looked older than his twenty-six years. Perhaps it was the restless, darting look in his eyes which gave that impression. When he stepped forward into the room it became apparent that the left sleeve of his jacket was empty.

"Am I interrupting?" he inquired lightly.

Benjamin Lassiter pushed back his chair and got to his feet.

"Rob!" he cried.

It was Robert, the youngest of the Lassiter children, the only son. He eyed him eagerly.

Then Benjamin Lassiter turned to the others. "Fellas," he said, clearing his throat significantly.

They had already edged toward the door.

"We see you at the Club or at City Hall?" Broderick asked.

Lassiter had put his sandwich down and was wiping his hands while he fondly studied his son's appearance.

"I'll call you," he told Broderick.

"Sure thing," blustered Broderick. " 'Bye, now. 'Bye,

Rob." He picked up his hat and went through the door, followed by Morse.

Malloy said, "You don't want me sticking around."

"No," Lassiter told him bluntly.

Hacker saw all three of them out.

Benjamin Lassiter was left alone with his son.

CHAPTER TEN:
FATHER AND SON

There was a long pause. The room seemed very quiet.

Then Benjamin said, "Well, did you see your mother?"

"Just to say 'Hello,' " Robert replied.

For a moment they remained silent, studying one another. Then, simultaneously, they both seemed to surrender to the irresistible. Each of them broke into a broad smile. They moved toward each other and threw their arms around each other. They clung tightly.

Then, as they separated, Benjamin said, "Every once in a while we can't help admitting who we are, can we?"

Robert cocked an eye at him. "Who we are?" he repeated.

Benjamin nodded.

"Father and son!" he said. He pronounced the words with tangible pride.

"I thought," Robert answered, "that you were going to say that we're Lassiters."

"Lassiters!" his father exclaimed. "God forbid! Too many Lassiters in the old country were hosrse thieves and—" he paused and grinned—"and politicians!" He rubbed his hands together. "Well!" he said. "What can I tell you, Rob?"

"What about the trip?" Robert asked. "Was it a good one?"

"We had a very nice trip. Your mother got around very well. No attacks. We enjoyed London very much. It's been shook up a bit. It got bombed by the zeppelins, you know."

"Yes," Robert said. "I know."

"I should have remembered," his father said ruefully. "You didn't lose that arm in the Meuse-Argonne for nothing. Anyway, Europe's nothing but a great big junkyard."

"Anything worth salvaging?" Robert asked lightly.

"Son, let me tell you this. A hell of a lot of Americans are going to get rich building up Europe again. If you ask me, that's going to be our principal business for maybe a whole generation to come. Hell, they haven't even got the straw to make bricks with!"

"Hmmm," Robert murmured, glancing toward the window. "You don't say, Daddy!"

Benjamin Lassiter had already sensed his son's diminishing interest in what he had to say. He went on, doing his best to spark Robert's interest.

"Yes!" he said, pounding his fist into the palm of his other hand. "The big money in America in *your* time will come out of two things that I can count. First, that one. I mean pouring capital into Europe and then taking it out again, multiplied times ten. Then there's opportunity number two: this thing that we put over on you boys while you were still too shell shocked to know what it was all about. I mean this joke called Prohibition."

Robert stared blankly at him.

"People are going to make money out of that?" he asked.

"They're already doing it."

"How?"

"Well, son, it's not so hard to figure out if you think about it. In Scotland, for instance, I bought the entire warehouse of Glencairn Scotch."

"What for?"

"What for? Why, they were ready to pour a half-million gallons of bonded stuff into the ocean. I took it off their hands at fourteen cents on the dollar. Can you imagine what we're going to make on that when they finally kill this idiotic law?" he demanded.

"They're going to kill it?"

"I give it two years at the most," Benjamin stated emphatically.

Robert threw himself into a chair and leaned back. He stifled a yawn, turning it into a strangled sigh. It was obvious that his mind was somewhere else.

"Rob?" his father said. He looked at him sharply.

"Huh?"

"You all right? I mean—"

Robert looked up at him and smiled.

"I'm fine," he said.

"Having fun?"

"You can call it that."

"I want you to get the best out of life," his father said. "I want you to have all the things—"

"I know," Robert said mildly. "All the things you missed out on. That's why you sent me to Milton Academy, moved heaven and earth to get me into Harvard. And that's why, when I wanted to get into the war, you called up Platt Andrew and got me into his ambulance corps."

"Well," his father said, "you didn't stay in that. You joined the American Army after we got into the war. That was what you wanted."

Robert shrugged. "I guess it was. Anyway," he added, glancing ruefully at his empty sleeve, "I didn't manage to stick with that very long either, did I?"

Quietly Lassiter asked, "Does it hurt anymore, son?"

"Pain's gone. Well, mostly all gone," Robert said. He winced, almost invisibly. Then he got to his feet. "Mama must be ready to receive me by now," he remarked. He made his way toward the door.

"Rob!" his father called out suddenly.

He stopped for an instant and turned his head.

"Yes?" he asked.

Benjamin Lassiter smiled at him.

"Son," he said, "be glad you're alive."

Robert stared in silence at his father, his hand on the doorknob.

Then he spoke.

"Why, Daddy?" he said.

He opened the door and went out, closing it behind him.

CHAPTER ELEVEN: MARY LASSITER TAKES A REST

Upstairs, just off the master bedroom, was a large bright room, full of sunshine, which was referred to by the staff as Mrs. Lassiter's morning room. She herself frequently observed that, with her health being what it was, it served, in actuality, as her morning, afternoon and evening room.

She was there now, her hat and furs and traveling clothes all removed and put away. She was stretched out on a satin-covered chaise longue, her gray hair combed out and pinned loosely into a comfortable chignon. A long-sleeved peignoir, generously trimmed with lace, hung in full folds around her slender body. The ebony cane leaned against the foot of the chaise. Pill bottles and a carafe of water stood on the table beside her.

Mrs. Hacker noiselessly came toward her, carrying an afghan which she tucked around Mrs. Lassiter's feet.

"Would you like me to draw the blinds now?" she asked.

"Not yet," Mrs. Lassiter said. "Why, I haven't really had a chance to look around me yet. How would I know I was home?" She cast her eyes contentedly around the room, taking in the soft colors, the pleasant furniture, the flowers set on the tables, the numberless family photographs framed in silver and set on every available surface and, finally, the portrait of her mother in its heavy gold frame, which hung over the marble fireplace. It was a rather academic and somewhat romanticized representation, with the old lady's white hair arranged in a modified pompadour, a black velvet ribbon around her neck and a wide fall of lace around her shoulders. Mary Lassiter was aware of how much the painter had flattered the builder's wife, but still she liked the picture. It was the way she liked to think her mother had been.

Marilyn Gardiner and Rosamond stood nearby, watching her solicitously.

"You really should take a nap now, Mama," Rosamond said. "You know that."

An impatient frown passed across her mother's forehead.

"That is true, Mrs. Lassiter," Miss Gardiner put in. "After the strain of getting home—"

Mrs. Lassiter disregarded the young women. She said, speaking to no one in particular, "Getting home is no strain. It's being away that takes it out of you." She turned to Mrs. Hacker. "The new girls look very nice," she remarked.

"They're good, obedient girls," Mrs. Hacker declared.

"How long do you think *these* will last?" Rosamond wanted to know.

"Ma'am?" Mrs. Hacker tucked the last loose end of the afghan into place under Mrs. Lassiter's slippers. "There," she said.

"Rosamond is right, Mrs. Hacker," Mary Lassiter affirmed. "You teach them and train them and give them a good trade, and the next thing you know, they'll be gallivanting off to greener fields."

"How many of these raw little girls have you brought over, Mrs. Hacker?" Rosamond asked her. "Have you ever stopped to count?"

"There were none during the war, Miss Rosamond," Mrs. Hacker reminded her defensively. "Remember that. None during the war."

"How many *since* the war?" Rosamond asked.

"I really haven't counted."

"How many?" Mary Lassiter insisted.

"Well, altogether, eleven," Mrs. Hacker admitted.

Mrs. Lassiter smiled.

"But Eleanor," Mrs. Hacker added hastily, "is sticking with us!"

There was a light tap on the door. A moment later Robert came into the room.

"Robby, darling!" Mary cried. "Come in. Come in!"

Miss Gardiner protested, "You really should try and get some rest!"

Mary Lassiter's eyes were full of life now. "I'm flat on me back, am I not? I'm restin', I'm restin'!" she cried out in a broad Irish accent.

Miss Gardiner and Rosamond exchanged a helpless glance.

"Come here, Robby," Mary Lassiter said, patting the chaise longue's apricot satin. "Sit down, sit down. Rosamond, go and lie down. You look tired. Miss Gardiner, where's my address book? Go write sweet little notes to all my friends. Tell them I'm home."

Rosamond gave her mother a quick peck on the cheek and departed. Marilyn found Mrs. Lassiter's brocade-covered address book and went out with it to write letters. Mrs. Hacker vanished inconspicuously.

Robert pulled up a small gilt chair beside the chaise longue and sat down.

The two of them regarded each other for a long speechless moment.

It was Mary who spoke first.

"It still hurts, doesn't it?" she said. "I can tell."

CHAPTER TWELVE:
EMILY HAS A PROBLEM

Emily Bullock had been waiting impatiently for her turn to see her father alone. She had a problem to discuss with him. Now that Robert had gone upstairs to see their mother, she had pushed her way into Benjamin Lassiter's study.

Without being asked, she poured two fingers of whisky into a tall glass and squirted several splashes of soda from the syphon over it. She sat down in a chair facing her father's.

Benjamin, frowning, said, "All right, Emily. What's on your mind?"

"It's Betsy," she said. "I'm worried about her."

"What's wrong with Betsy? She looked all right to me," he said. He picked up his unfinished steak tartare sandwich and bit into it.

Emily waited while he finished his mouthful and wiped his lips with a napkin.

"She's seeing someone," she said at last, shrilly.

Benjamin pushed away the rest of his sandwich. He suddenly didn't feel hungry anymore.

"Father," Emily said in that emphatic way of hers which always fussed him, "it's just too mysterious!"

"Why mysterious?" he countered. "The girl is old enough to go out with boys."

Emily took a quick gulp of her drink. Then she shook her head. The shiny feathers on her hat trembled. "With *what* boys?" she demanded. "She's been *seeing* somebody—*some*body, Father—three, four, five nights a week. And she simply will not tell us who it is! Trev is wild. And she's neglecting her studies. She comes home at eleven, sometimes even at twelve o'clock at night, virtually mashed to a pulp. And when I ask her where she's been, she says what right have I to cross-examine her?" Emily firmed her mouth into a hard bitter line. "It's obviously somebody we wouldn't approve of," she went on, "or she wouldn't keep it such a damned secret."

"Maybe," Lassiter suggested quietly, "that's because it's her own damned business."

"And I," Emily replied savagely, taking another gulp of her scotch and soda, "am her own damned mother!"

Benjamin Lassiter leaned forward in his chair.

"Tell me something, Emily," he began.

"What?"

"Since when have you taken to drinking before dinner?"

She eyed her father coldly.

"Ever since I started to *enjoy* drinking," she replied. "It took me years."

There was a silence. They regarded each other warily. It suddenly occurred to Benjamin to ask himself if this hard elegant creature sitting opposite him was his daughter Emily or some woman named Mrs. Trevor Bullock, a strange society matron whom he hardly knew.

Suddenly Emily was saying, "I want to tell you something, Daddy."

"What?" he asked guardedly.

"I'm going to suggest to Trev that we call in one of those detective agencies."

"Don't you dare!" he burst out savagely. He rose to his feet. "Don't you dare, Emily!" he repeated.

She was taken aback by the violence of his reaction.

"Why?" she gasped.

"We don't set spies on one another," he announced in a voice from which the anger had not subsided. "Not in this family! Leave the girl alone. We'll find out soon enough what this is all about."

"You mean," Emily snapped back at him, "*you'll* find out?"

"I mean," he replied, biting off his words, "leave her alone." He paused and regarded his daughter, sitting there with her beautiful face frozen into petulance and discontent under the elegant feathered helmet, her slender fingers clutching the highball glass. "There's one thing you have to realize, Emily," he said at last.

She raised her eyes defiantly to his.

"And what's that, Daddy?" she demanded.

"Simply this," he said. "Your daughter Betsy is eighteen years old."

CHAPTER THIRTEEN: BIRDCAGES

Of the Lassiter staff, only the Hackers and Miss Gardiner lived in the house on Louisburg Square. Marilyn Gardiner had a small bedroom decorated with floral wallpaper on the top floor of the house. The Hackers had their own suite: a living room and a bedroom, divided by portieres of glass beads.

Emmeline Hacker had made it cosy enough so that when the door was closed she and Arthur felt comparatively isolated, cut off from the activity of the rest of the house. It was almost like having their own apartment, their own home—something they had always longed for and frequently talked about when they were alone. Most of the furniture had been there when they came, relics of the house in which Mary Lassiter had been brought up. It consisted chiefly of heavy pieces of mission oak, but Emmeline Hacker's deft hands had crocheted an army of doilies and antimacassars and embroidered flocks of cushion covers which were strewn over everything. Their wedding picture and a photograph of Hacker in his Rifle Brigade uniform were displayed on the dark mantelpiece. The lower section of the mantelpiece was covered with bilious green tiles against which a cheerful gas grate burned. The Hacker's sitting room was always kept very warm. This was because of Mrs. Hacker's potted plants, chiefly ferns. They lined all the windows. But even more important than Mrs. Hacker's plant pots were Mr. Hacker's cages.

The room was filled with birdcages and twittering canaries. They were Hacker's private passion.

Hacker had stolen a moment to see how the two baby canaries which had recently been hatched from eggs were getting along.

He found his wife was already there, standing by the window, thoughtfully staring out at the rooftops of Beacon Hill.

Hacker went over at once to the nursery cage. The two fledglings were in their nest, screaming for sustenance. He peered into the cage, making chirping sounds with his pursed lips while the mother bird flitted from perch to perch.

"I had to get the father out of there," he remarked to Mrs. Hacker. "He was acting very strangely. I guess the male birds get jealous."

Mrs. Hacker did not reply. She continued to gaze out of the window.

When Hacker had finished feeding the young ones, he turned to his wife.

"Who's with him now?" he asked.

"Miss Rosamond," Mrs. Hacker told him.

"And Mr. Robert?"

"What about Mr. Robert?"

"I mean, did he leave with a smile or a frown?"

"It's hard to tell with Mr. Robert," she said.

"Miss Emily?"

"With a frown."

Hacker considered, his eyes raking the birdcage to make sure that nothing else was required.

"Then who's next?" he asked, poking a bit of lettuce between the bars of the cage.

"I am," she said.

He jerked his head quickly in her direction.

"Not today, love," he said. "The man has just come home."

"I know," she replied. "But we must not lose *any* time." She sighed and let the muslin curtain fall. She straightened her shoulders. "I'm going to him now. Miss Rosamond will have had her little say."

Hacker stared helplessly at her. Then he shrugged and turned his attention back to the canaries. There was never much time, he thought, for his birdcages. Still, he reflected, as he heard Mrs. Hacker's brisk footsteps departing, it might have been better if she'd waited a day or two to tell him. You never knew how Mr. Lassiter would react to something like that.

CHAPTER FOURTEEN: MRS. HACKER'S FIVE MINUTES

It was Rosamond's turn with her father.

Emily had brushed past her when she left without even saying a word of goodbye. Well, she was used to Emily and her ways. And Emily, when she didn't get exactly what she wanted, could be—well, trying. You'd have thought that, married to Trevor Bullock and with those nice children, and always such a beauty, Emily would have been less discontented and more—sisterly? Still, the house seemed calmer with Emily out of it, and Rosamond had so much to discuss with her father. She was sure that he would be pleased with the way she had looked after things for him while he was away in Europe.

So now she sat on a low chair with sheets of paper all over her lap. She had already been there for at least ten precious minutes of Daddy's time, referring to those papers and reading to him from some of them.

"The house in Newport," she went on, sounding very businesslike, "is taking the winter weather very nicely. No pipes frozen, and you'll be glad to hear that the leak in the orangerie has been traced and fixed. Now we come to Palm Beach. Mr. Oberdorf suggests that he market the oranges next year, we've gotten so many." She riffled the papers. "Now—" she went on.

Benjamin Lassiter stretched and yawned.

"Baby," he said, "I'm tired."

"Oh, Daddy!" Rosamond exclaimed hastily. "I'm sorry." She gathered her papers together and sprang to her feet. "Of course you're tired. I should have thought." She bent over and kissed his forehead. "Tomorrow?"

"Bright and early," he said.

"Promise?"

"I promise."

"Good!" she cried. She scudded toward the door.

"Listen, Roz," Benjamin called after her. "I have a thought."

She stopped and turned.

"What, Daddy?" she asked eagerly.

He made a tent of the fingers of both hands and frowned down at it. "I'm told that the whole town is going to go crazy on Friday night," he said.

"Oh," she answered brightly. "Have you heard? It's down with Bacchus! Up with Prohibition! Yes, I imagine the whole country will just be one big madhouse."

Benjamin Lassiter continued to regard his tented fingers. "Well, this is just a thought. We've come home, and that's an occasion for a celebration. It's a good excuse to get the whole family together." He broke up the tent, spread out his hands and peered up at her. "Why don't we do it Friday night, and make believe the whole world is celebrating my return from Europe?"

Efficiency swept over Rosamond at once. "A dinner party Friday night," she said. "Good. I'll make the arrangements."

She flew to the door and opened it.

Mrs. Hacker and Harry Emmet, the chauffeur, were standing in the foyer outside. As Rosamond dashed past them, Benjamin called through the open door, "D'you want to see me, Mrs. Hacker?"

"Please, Mr. Lassiter," she said.

"In a few minutes then," he told her. He nodded to Emmet, who went in, closed the door behind him, and remained standing.

He was more than the official family chauffeur, and he knew it. Unofficially, he took care of any special jobs that Benjamin Lassiter needed doing and which were too confidential for Marvin Malloy to attend to. He was good looking, and his smart uniform with its bright buttons and high laced boots gave an added cockiness to his appearance. His dark hair was carefully combed. He had neat crisp ears and a loose mouth which, when there was no cigarillo sticking jauntily out of it, was twisted into a faintly mocking smile. Emmet was in his thirties. He had tried a number of jobs before settling down as the Lassiters' chauffeur, jobs that he usually referred to with a significant wink as "kicking around the world a bit, seeing a bit of life, you know."

"Well?" Benjamin Lassiter said.

Emmet whipped off the leather-peaked cap which perched on the back of his head. He grinned.

"No complaints, Mr. Lassiter," he said.

Lassiter instinctively lowered his voice.

"Been keeping an eye on him?" he asked.

"Like you said, Mr. Lassiter," Emmet replied breezily. "I'm around whenever he needs me."

"What about his health? It seems good."

Emmet considered.

"His arm hurts him once in a while, but less and less, I think," he said.

"And his state of mind?" Lassiter asked, narrowing his eyes.

Again Emmet considered. Then he flashed a quick grin. "Well," he said, "he's not exactly a kewpie doll, but I think he's getting better. We got to be patient with our soldier boys, huh, Mr. Lassiter?"

Lassiter disregarded the last remark. Emmet's grin disappeared as quickly as it came.

"He doesn't know I asked you to look after him—" Lassiter began.

"No, *sir!*" Emmet's reply was quick and emphatic.

"That's important," Lassiter said.

"I never let on," Emmet reassured him. "Never, Mr. Lassiter."

"All right," Lassiter told him, "there's just one more thing. My granddaughter, Miss Betsy, appears to be seeing someone. I want you to find out who it is."

"Yes, sir," Emmet replied rather too quickly and, accepting his dismissal, jerked his hand in a brisk half-salute, tilted his cap back on his head and went to the door.

Mrs. Hacker was still waiting outside it when he opened it and swaggered past her.

"Please come in, Mrs. Hacker," Lassiter told her.

Tight-lipped, Mrs. Hacker came into the room and closed the door behind her. She stood with her back to it, her hands clasped at her waist.

"I would appreciate five minutes, sir," she announced gravely.

"Then you shall have them, Mrs. Hacker," he said, wondering vaguely what was on her mind. Mrs. Hacker seldom made demands on his time: she and Hacker between them ran the house with a minimum of fuss and hardly ever disturbed him with their problems, which was the way he liked things to be. "Sit down, please," he said, aware of the special solemnity of the occasion.

They both sat down, she on the edge of her chair.

He waited.

Mrs. Hacker stared at the carpet. There was a thread at her feet. She would have to speak to Eleanor about that.

Then she tore her gaze from the offending bit of thread and began nervously.

"Mr. Lassiter," she said, "in your absence, apart from the new girls, I have taken the liberty of bringing over one more member of the family."

"Yes?" he said, noncommittally, and continued to wait.

"It's me sister Kathleen's son, Brian," she said.

"When is he coming?"

"He's here."

"Here in this house?"

She shook her head. "Here in Boston, Mr. Lassiter," she said. "He is here in Boston."

"Oh."

She paused. Then she added, "He's in custody."

Lassiter frowned.

"Whose custody?" he demanded.

Mrs. Hacker bridled slightly.

"All his papers are in order, sir," she said.

"Who's holding him in custody?" Lassiter persisted.

"He is in excellent health," Mrs. Hacker rushed on in a tight voice. "He has all his teeth, no diseases of eye, ear, nose or—"

"Mrs. Hacker," Lassiter told her abruptly, "if it is only five minutes you want, we are wasting time."

Mrs. Hacker took a deep breath. She bit her lips hard, fighting back the welling imminent tears.

She said, "The Customs people have discovered that he spent some time in jail."

"In jail," he repeated.

"In Limerick," she added.

He leaned back and surveyed her. "Ah," he said.

Her voice rose almost to a wail. "Mr. Lassiter, they're going to send him back!"

She found a handkerchief and pressed her nose into it. Mr. Lassiter sat there and let her weep silently for a moment or two.

After a while he said, "All right, Mrs. Hacker. What'd he do? Steal? Kill?"

Mrs. Hacker's back straightened up at once. The handkerchief disappeared. "He's a good, decent boy!" she maintained, her eyes flashing. "He's got an education and a wonderful gift of the tongue! You should hear him make a speech!"

"Is that what they sent him to jail for?" Lassiter cut in.

She raised her head and looked him squarely in the eye.

"It was for a political offense!" she said.

"And what was the nature of it?"

"In Easter week of '17, during the English War, he marched in a parade."

Lassiter weighed the information.

"What else did he do, Mrs. Hacker?" he inquired.

In a somewhat subdued voice, she answered, "He threw a stone."

"I see. Hit anybody?"

"Only a constable," said Mrs. Hacker.

"Ah." Lassiter paused. Again he made a tent of his fingers and contemplated it. "And it was just a stone?" he asked, raising his eyes to hers finally. "You're sure it wasn't a rock? Or a brick?"

"Nobody was harmed!" Mrs. Hacker flashed back. "For some slight injury to the constable's pride, Brian was given three months in the workhouse. That's English justice for you! And now they've found out about it in the Customs and they are going to deport the boy!"

"If he's got a political record," Lassiter told her reasonably, "they've got every right to do that."

"He's no criminal!" she protested hotly. "His papers are completely in order! I ask you, Mr. Lassiter, would the Irish government give him a clean bill of health on his passport if he was a criminal?"

"They do that sometimes," he told her, "when they're

really anxious to get rid of somebody. They just fob him off on another country."

"Mr. Lassiter," she cried, wringing her hands. "Have mercy on the boy! They're going to send him back to Ireland!"

"And what's so godawful about that?" he asked. "From what they tell me, Ireland must be heaven. Why, my own mother—"

Mrs. Hacker looked at him in anguish. "Mr. Lassiter, please!"

Mr. Lassiter sighed. He gave her a quick nod. Then he reached out and picked up the telephone.

Mrs. Hacker shot him a grateful glance. Her five minutes were up, she knew. But she had gotten what she wanted. Without waiting to listen to Mr. Lassiter's conversation with the men at the Customs House, she glided quietly out of the room to tell her husband.

CHAPTER FIFTEEN: BRIAN

The living room of the Lassiters' house on Louisburg Square was unlike those of its neighbors in that it lacked their richly austere Colonial look. It contained no inherited Hepplewhite highboys, no Lowestoft bowls or Paul Revere silver. The paintings on the wall were not by Copley or Gilbert Stuart, but, rather, landscapes vaguely of the Barbizon school, seemingly executed in brown gravy, protected by glass and surrounded by wide gilt frames with little lights set over them.

It was an immense room, stuffy, comfortable and filled with heavy pieces of furniture. The bibelots it contained were obviously expensive, but overly ornate in style. Nothing in it had been changed since Benjamin Lassiter bought the house and moved his family into it.

Mrs. Hacker sat rigidly on a sofa, her knees pressed primly together. Her hands were folded in her lap, but they did not remain at rest. She nervously twiddled her wedding ring with her fingers.

She was not alone in the room.

A slim young man, with wild, curly, brown hair was wandering about in it, curiously examining its contents.

He had on a pair of shabby but clean corduroy trousers, a shapeless Donegal tweed jacket and a neatly buttoned vest. His shirt was clean, his necktie slightly raveled but respectable, and over his shoulders a knitted scarf had been carelessly flung, almost, it would seem, as a gesture of defiance to the world at large and to the Lassiters in particular. He held a cloth cap in his hands.

"Will you please sit down?" Mrs. Hacker cried at last, in exasperation.

For this was her nephew, Brian Mallory, released from the custody of the immigration officials at the Customs House and now in hers.

He disregarded her plea and continued to stare at everything with his intense light eyes.

He paused now and stood in front of the mantelpiece, glancing up at an impressively framed portrait of a stern old gentleman with heavy jowls and a pair of shewd small eyes.

"And who's this one?" Brian demanded. His voice was light and mocking, with an unmistakably Irish accent to it.

"That's Mrs. Lassiter's father," his aunt informed him.

Brian Màllory continued to peer speculatively at the picture.

"Oh," he said. "The brickmaker."

Mrs. Hacker pursed her lips. "The brickmaker who made ten million dollars," she said.

Brian eyed the old man's rigid face for an instant or two longer.

"He don't look that rich to me," he remarked, finally.

"Keep your voice down, will you!" she told him, glancing nervously toward the door.

He wandered over to a table and picked up a large piece of carved Chinese jade from its teakwood stand.

"Now *that* looks rich," he said. He hefted it. He grinned impishly at her. "D'you think they'd ever miss it?"

"Brian!"

He laughed and put it down. Then he picked up a photograph in a silver frame and studied it. He turned to his aunt with a questioning look.

"The Palmer children," she told him. "Daughter Maude's children."

He delivered his judgment. "A proper pack of monkeys," he said.

"Brian!" she cried. "For heaven's sake!"

Disregarding her protests, he grabbed another photograph and examined the faces in it.

"And these," he said, "must be the daughters." He waved the frame in the air. "The four department store dummies," he remarked, his lips curled into a sneer.

Mrs. Hacker bridled.

"I'll have you know," she said, "that the Lassiter sisters are known for their beauty! They're famous all over Boston for it!" She lowered her voice. "Three of them, anyhow," she added.

"A decent percentage," he admitted. He set the picture down and picked up another. He held it out toward her. "Which beauty is this?"

"That one's Fawn."

He thoughtfully regarded the sepia-tinted photograph and clucked his tongue impudently at it.

"Brian," Mrs. Hacker cried out in exasperation. "You're enough to try the patience of a saint. Will you do as I tell you? Just sit down here next to me and keep your mouth shut!"

"Easy, Aunt Emmeline," he said. "Easy, now. We're all friends here. Nobody's on trial."

A voice cut quietly across the room. "Not yet," it said.

Benjamin Lassiter stood in the entranceway.

Mrs. Hacker rose to her feet instantly. She stood there, flustered.

"Oh, Mr. Lassiter!" she gasped. "I didn't hear you

come into the room. Mr. Lassiter, this is the boy, Brian. Brian Mallory, my sister's boy."

"How are you, Brian?" Lassiter asked.

Up until this moment Brian had merely been behaving like a cocksure young man in his twenties with a loose, devil-may-care style. Now, confronting Benjamin Lassiter, he was suddenly galvanized into another character. A wide grin of boyish innocence creased his face and his light Irish lilt grew stronger so that it was almost like singing.

"Oh, thank you, Mr. Lassiter," he said, his eyes wide and boyish. "I'm very well. Very well, indeed!"

Mrs. Hacker jostled his elbow.

"Well!" she said. "Go forward. Shake the man's hand!"

Brian fumbled at his cap and lowered his eyes in a show of youthful embarrassment.

"Oh," he said. "Is that the way it's done, now? Well, then, I'm glad to."

He ambled across the room with his hand outstretched.

"How do you do, sir!" he cried.

"How do you do," Benjamin replied.

"If me manners leave something to be desired, sir," Brian went on, "remember, sir, I'm only a country lout."

"Drop it, Brian," Benjamin said sharply, and without shaking the proffered hand went over to a large upright chair and sat down.

"I'm a country boy myself," he went on. "That makes me immune to the blarney of country louts." He looked up at the boy. He was not smiling. "Didn't your aunt tell you that?"

Brian remained frozen in his place. His jaw hung slack. He stared at Lassiter.

Mrs. Hacker raised her chin and flung a smug smile in her nephew's direction, a smile which stated as clearly as though she had spoken the words, "I told you so!"

"Sit down, Brian," Benjamin ordered.

Subdued now, Brian lowered himself cautiously into the closest chair.

"I hear you're a spellbinder," Lassiter told him. He leaned back. "Make me a speech," he commanded.

"I've just been slapped hard, sir," Brian said, with only a flicker of his former jauntiness. "I'm taking time to reel from the blow."

"*Roll* with it, boy," Benjamin said.

Brian braced himself. "All right, then," he answered. "Here goes." He took a deep breath. "I am in your debt, sir, for disinvolving me with the idiots at the Customs, and I am grateful." He paused and glanced up at Lassiter. "How's that?" he asked.

"Good," Benjamin replied with a quick nod. "Anyway, it's better. It's better than that attempt to *charm* me to death. Now let's get on with it. You got into some trouble back home?"

"Yes!" Brian's expression became expansive again. "Well, sir," he began.

"I just want the facts," Benjamin informed him in a low, level voice. "That's all I want to hear. No poetry. No Irish lullabies."

For a long moment Brian stared at him. Then he lowered his eyes.

"I hit this cop with a brick," he said.

"Why?"

"Because he was a cop."

"Now, *that's* poetic!" Lassiter remarked drily. There was a long pause, during which the older man continued to take the measure of the young newcomer. "What are your plans?" he asked at last.

Mrs. Hacker moved forward. "I was wondering, sir, till he catched his breath, if—"

Benjamin Lassiter kept his glance fixed on Brian.

"What's your trade?" he asked brusquely.

"Well!" Brian expelled a long breath. "Me natural genius, just like yourself, sir, is for politics," he said.

Lassiter continued to regard him steadily.

"What's your trade?" he repeated.

Brain had to take a deep gulp of air before he could steel himself to tell the truth.

"Me father was the best maker of stone walls in the county," he admitted. "I was brought up in the trade."

Lassiter considered.

"Stone walls," he repeated.

Then he nodded.

"Boston has been *waiting* for you, young man," he commented in a wry tone. He got to his feet then. "Well," he said, "make yourself at home. You're welcome to stay for as long as it takes you to catch your breath." He nodded to Brian's aunt. "It's all right, Mrs. Hacker," he said.

She flashed him a grateful smile. Before she could say anything, he had shaken Brian's hand and left the room.

Brian stood staring after him.

"Well, now!" Mrs. Hacker said.

"Masterful!" Brian exclaimed.

"What?"

"Did you see that? He had me on me back in five seconds. Then he kept me there for the next five minutes. Beautiful it was, beautiful!"

"I told you!" Mrs. Hacker reminded him. "He is the smart one, isn't he?"

Brian wasn't listening to her. He was lost in his own thoughts.

"*Isn't* he though?" Mrs. Hacker repeated.

But Brian still seemed unaware of what she had said. He remained staring at the doorway through which Benjamin Lassiter had just passed.

"Who the *hell,*" he remarked thoughtfully, "does he put me in mind of?"

CHAPTER SIXTEEN: FLICKERING SHADOWS

Robert Lassiter had a bedroom and a little sitting room of his own on the second floor of the house, facing the back. They were curiously barren rooms, both of them. The walls were absolutely bare of pictures. The bookshelves were empty. There were no relics of his boyhood to be seen anywhere: none of the usual detritus of school and college. Nor was there anything in evidence to account for the time which he had spent in France, first as a volunteer with Platt Andrew's American ambulance unit and later in the uniform of the A.E.F.

The actual furnishings were at a minimum. A couple of old chairs stood on either side of the vacant fireplace. There were some scarred and battered tables, a nondescript desk. And that was all.

Robert sat staring out of the window.

Dully, he viewed the gritty, gray New England sky. The light was fading. It was the hour when daylight was drawing to an end, the hour just before it was time to turn on the lamps in the streets of Boston. He could hear the muffled sounds of activity in the house around him, but he was indifferent to them.

He was indifferent, in fact, to everything, even to the glass which he held in his hand.

There was a whisky bottle and a bucket half-filled with ice on the low table beside him. He took a long slow sip of his drink. He wasn't even sure that he cared for that anymore.

His hooded eyes traveled deliberately from the window to the table. For a long moment he studied the bottle and the ice bucket, peering at them as though he had never seen them before. Then, calmly, with a sweep of his arm, he knocked the bucket off the table. Water sloshed over the carpet and crushed ice rolled across the floor.

He stared in silence at the overturned crystal bucket and at the scattered bits of ice.

After what seemed a very long time there was a knock on the door.

"Come!" he called. He knew that it was his own voice, but it didn't particularly sound like it.

Rosamond dashed in.

"I heard a—" she began. Then she caught sight of the melting ice. "Oh, Rob!" she exclaimed.

She hurriedly crossed the room to where he sat. She knelt down and started to gather the scattered ice, putting it back in the bucket.

"You've made such a mess!" she complained. "It's going to melt and start soaking through!"

Her surveyed her calmly, as though watching her from very far away.

"Never call the servants, Roz," he remarked languidly, at last. "Do the dirty work yourself, huh?"

Without answering him, she straightened up and took the ice bucket into the adjoining room. He could hear the ice being dumped into the toilet, followed by the sound of the toilet being flushed.

Rosamond returned.

"Shall I chop some more ice for you?" she asked.

"No!" he answered curtly. "Get somebody else to do it."

"Do you want me to do anything for you?" She stood there, regarding him uncertainly.

"Yes," he said.

"What?"

"Sit down, Roz." He waved vaguely at the chair opposite him. "Talk to me."

Rosamond perched on the edge of the chair, tucking her skirt fussily around her.

"Well," he said, "come on. Talk to me. I'm not so goddamned blotto that I can't hold a conversation."

"You never are," she said.

He raised his glass to her.

"Always appreciate a compliment!" he remarked. He took a long gulp of his drink.

"What shall we talk about?" Rosamond asked, her voice determinedly chatty. "Are you happy that Mama and Daddy are back home?"

"Delirious," he said.

She said, her face flushed and her shoulders squirming self-consciously, "Rob, you must stop *staring* at me!"

"Oh," he said, still staring, "sorry."

"Well, then stop."

"I was just trying to see *inside* of you, Roz," he said.

"Why? Can't you stand the outside?"

"Oh, cut it out, Roz," he told her sharply. "All I'm thinking is, how a girl like you, bright and smart, a *wonderful* girl, doesn't do anything with herself!"

She stared back at him for a moment. Then she smiled.

"Robby," she said suddenly.

"What?"

"Why don't you get out of this room? Get up and out?"

"Out to what?"

"Oh, I don't know. Out to anything. Join the Navy and see the world! Why don't you, Rob?"

He raised his empty sleeve at her.

"For a damned good reason!" he said. "Now, what's yours?"

She shook her head. "I simply don't understand you, Rob," she said, pleadingly. "Why does that empty sleeve drive you into yourself? Why does it make you so rude and bitter and mean to people? Why should an empty sleeve keep you sitting in this dreary room all day long?"

He cast his dull eyes around the room.

"Because it's ugly!" he said.

She smiled at him. Her smile was her unspoken answer to his question.

He glared fuzzily at her for a moment, before understanding the point she had made. Then, when he got her drift, he was ashamed.

"Come on, Roz," he said. "*That's* not your problem."

"Isn't it?"

"For God's sake!" he replied. "You're not such a bad-looking girl, Roz. Come on!"

Rosamond's smile turned rueful.

"I might have gotten used to my face," she went on, "if I hadn't been brought up in this family. You've seen it, Rob! Don't deny it! The look on people's faces when they suddenly discover that I'm the fourth Lassiter sister. 'Oh, I didn't know that there were *four* of you! You certainly don't look like—' " She broke off, shaking her head abruptly. "It's one thing being born plain," she resumed. "Most people are. It's quite something else when you've got to stand up next to three older sisters who look like Maude and Emily and Fawn."

"Oh, come on, Roz," he said joshingly. "What about Cinderella?"

She burst into a peal of laughter. "That's a terrible comparison!" she exclaimed. "Cinderella was a pretty girl! It was the sisters who were ugly!"

Suddenly Robert rose. He set his glass down, carefully

making sure that it stood on its base. Then he walked stiffly toward the door.

"Where are you going?" Rosamond called after him.

"Out," he said. "Out of here. Out to see the world!"

He was gone.

Rosamond lingered in the bare, bleak room. Outside, the twilight was deepening. Soon it would be time to light the lamps. Abruptly, under her breath, she began to hum an old tune, "Just A Song At Twilight," but as abruptly stopped as she recalled the words about love's old sweet song.

She got up, patted her soft hair to make sure it was in order. Then she hurried out of the empty twilit room.

CHAPTER SEVENTEEN: TURNING DOWN THE BEDS

In the master bedroom, the new maids, Katie and Maureen, were turning down the beds.

They worked together, but rather awkwardly, like two young horses not used to being hitched in the same harness.

"No," Katie protested. "No, no! That's not the way, Maureen. We're supposed to lift it at the same time. There. That's right. Fold it down to the bottom. Right! Now—" She looked across at Maureen and frowned. "What did Eleanor say to do now?"

"Lift your end," Maureen directed. "That's it. Now tuck it under. There's the coverlet."

"Coverlet!" Katie echoed. "That's the word I was trying to remember." She folded her end and let out a sharp sigh of satisfaction. "And r-i-i-i-ight you are!" She shook her head. You're a good deal smarter than I am, Maureen," she admitted.

Maureen permitted herself a toss of the head, knocking her cap slightly askew.

"At some things, yes," she answered pertly.

"Well!" said Katie. "That's a nasty thing to say now! You—"

Whatever Katie was about to say died on her lips. Maureen was staring, her mouth open like a carp's, over Katie's shoulder. Kate turned to follow Maureen's startled gaze.

A young man with curly hair and bright searching eyes and dressed in Old Country clothes, as they could plainly see, had just walked into Mrs. Lassiter's morning room from the hallway, as cool as you please. The door was still open behind him.

"What are you doing in here?" Katie called out.

"You have no business in here!" Maureen declared, shocked.

The young man swaggered forward.

"One of you is Kate and one of you is Maureen," he said. "Which is which I can't recall. Identify yourselves!"

Maureen wasn't at all sure she liked the impertinent air of him. "Stay out of here!" she warned. "I'll take the poker to you!"

But he only came closer, bold as they come, as Maureen told herself. He pointed to the beds.

"One for him, and one for her," he said with a snigger. "Is that the way it is here in Boston?"

Maureen glared at him. It was Katie who answered.

"Yes," she said.

"And if he wants to tickle her," he went on, "he has to reach over. Is that it?"

Katie ducked her head and clapped a hand over her mouth, but a giggle escaped.

Maureen turned to her indignantly.

"Don't start laughing at him!" she said harshly.

He regarded the beds ruefully.

"Is that what happens to all Irishmen once they become Americans?" he demanded with a mournful shake of his head.

The girls goggled at him.

Before either of them could reply, a voice inquired from the other room, "What is going on?"

All three of them turned to see who it was.

Rosamond had just entered her mother's morning room from the hallway. The girls eyed her, terror-stricken, as she moved forward to the doorway of the bedroom.

"All right," she said briskly. "You've turned the beds down. All right. Now go on to Mr. Robert's room."

Maureen and Katie scuttled out in a flutter of caps and apron strings. The young man seemed in no hurry whatever to depart.

Rosamond stared at him in her slightly nearsighted way.

"You must be Mrs. Hacker's nephew," she said.

"Brian Mallory, in the flesh," he said, swaggering at her. "And what are you, may I ask? Second in command, like that?" He appraised her unabashedly and coolly. "You must be the girl Eleanor I've been hearing about." Without waiting for her to answer, he jerked his thumb at the beds. "Now," he demanded, "what the hell does that mean, 'turned down'? What's it mean, 'the beds are turned down'?"

"What are you doing in here?" Rosamond asked.

"Two girls to pull down the blankets like that?" he said, keeping his eyes on hers. "They can't do a thing like that themselves? I suppose that they have to have somebody to feed them, too? And who is it who lifts the silver spoon to their mouths?"

Rosamond stood there, too astonished at his cheekiness to reply.

He swung around and peered curiously into the bathroom.

Rosamond found her voice at last.

"Mr. Mallory," she said, "what are you doing in this room?"

With his hands high on the doorjamb, he leaned into the bathroom.

"Then there's the ablutions," he went on, his voice high and mocking. "Tell me, who is it does for them when it comes to—"

"Mr. Mallory," Rosamond cried. "Please!"

He swung around.

"The way you talk, you must have been born here," he said. "Where did your people come from? From the hoity-toity air of you, I'd say it was Dublin."

Rosamond bravely restrained herself from stamping her foot.

"Answer me, Mr. Mallory!"

He could see that she was really angry now. That seemed to appease him.

"All right," he said, laughing. "All right! I was in the hallway giving myself a bit of a walk. You might say that I was examining the house."

Her eyes blazed. "And what right have you to—"

He considered her. "Katie has the face of a little cat," he remarked thoughtfully, "and Maureen has the face of a bird. Yours is the face of a great angry rose."

If he had meant to disarm her with that, he had not succeeded.

She eyed him coldly.

"Mr. Mallory," she said, "just make things easy for all of us. Take your big mouth and your enormous gall out of here before somebody walks in and there is hell to pay."

He merely stood there, considering.

"Dublin, all right!" he said at last. "What else? The sacred and the profane in one withering breath! Admit it, now. Your old man came from Dublin."

"If you must know," she replied angrily, "my grandfather came from Galway, which is around the world from Dublin, Now. Mr. Mallory!"

In a flash he leaped onto one of the beds and lay stretched out on it.

Rosamond gasped.

"What are you?"

He patted the bed. "Come on," he said in a sly coaxing voice. "It's very comfortable."

"Get up, you idiot!" she ordered. She was beside herself. "Are you crazy?"

But he did not get up. Instead, he reached out and grabbed her, pulling her down beside him. She thrashed about wildly in his grasp. He was thin, but his arms were strong and he held her there easily, with a smile on his lips as he bent over her. Then his hand was on her face, twisting it toward his for a kiss.

Suddenly he clamped his hand across her mouth and held her down, helplessly rigid, on the bed. The smile was frozen on his face.

At that moment Rosamond too, through her panic, could make out the voices in the hallway outside.

Beyond the open door of the morning room the voices grew louder. She could distinctly hear Eleanor instructing Kate and Maureen. "But you must learn to leave the window just slightly open in Miss Rosamond's room. The mistress likes the windows closed."

At that point Eleanor and the two girls passed the open doorway. Neither Rosamond nor Brian could see them; the wall blocked their view. They lay there on the bed, Rosamond not daring to struggle. From the clear sound of Eleanor's voice it was evident now that the maids had gone past the doorway, but Brian and Rosamond remained there, locked together, panting. Rosamond could feel the boy's warm breath on her face. It burned her cheeks.

Maureen suddenly popped back and stuck her snub nose past the jamb for a quick look around. She could see nothing, fortunately, because the beds were just out of range of the door. Then, with a shrug, she moved on to join the others.

Rosamond could hear Eleanor's voice fading away. "And now, if the two of you will follow me, I'll show you where the bed linen is kept. I don't know why Mrs. Hacker has never—"

Eleanor's voice diminished into silence. Their footsteps passed out of hearing range.

The danger was over.

Or was it? For Brian's face was still pressed close to hers. He was looking down at her. His hand was still there, covering her mouth. When he spoke it was in a quick confidential whisper.

"I was just playing games," he said. "Don't hang me for it." He paused, his light flecked eyes peering into hers. Then he spoke her name. "Roz," he said. "Is that what they call you? Or is it Rosie?"

A tremor of shock passed over her, chasing the anger from her eyes.

He slowly released the pressure of his hand on her mouth.

She lay there, motionless, staring at him in stupefaction. He had known all the time who she was. He had never, not for a moment really, mistaken her for Eleanor.

And now he let go his iron grip on her body. Rosamond jumped from the bed and leaned against the wall. She felt limp. Her bones had turned to rubber. She was breathing hard.

Slowly, nonchalantly, Brian got off the bed. He moved swiftly into the morning room. At the door he turned to her.

"You can holler for help now," he told her. There was that smile again, the smile she could have wrenched from his face. "Rosie," he said, tossing her name at her as though it were a wilted flower. Then he vanished into the hallway.

Rosamond remained with her back to the wall, staring toward the open doorway. She was still panting from exhaustion and outrage. With a shudder, she turned to the bed. It was a show of untidy telltale wrinkles. Frantically she smoothed it out.

She straightened up again after repairing the damage as best she could. She turned and looked toward the door once more.

"You can holler for help now." That was what he had said before vanishing, along with that impudent, maddening, cocksure Irish smile of his. She could have ground his face with its smile into the floor with her heel. Damn his insolence!

After an interval she drew her hands over her hair, pushing it back into place and jabbing the straggling hairpins back where they belonged. Then she pressed her fingers against her trembling lips.

"Help," she whispered softly.

CHAPTER EIGHTEEN: A LITTLE GAME OF POKER

A checkered cloth covered the round table in the corner of the kitchen. An overhead lamp threw a steady glow over it, flooding with light the bottles, the glasses, the cards and the chips.

It was Tuesday night, and the usual weekly little game of poker was in progress.

There were five of them playing: the Hackers, Emmet, O'Hara and Piper. Mrs. Hacker had a heavy cardigan over her housekeeper's dress. Hacker, as usual, wore his jacket and tie. O'Hara was in shirtsleeves and vest, revealing the elastic garters he wore above the elbows to keep his sleeves up. Piper was still in his white uniform, the large napkin still tied around his neck, although he had removed his cap. Emmet was not in uniform. His necktie hung loose and he chewed on one of the big cigars from the humidor in Mr. Lassiter's study.

Emmet smiled pleasantly as he studied the hand of cards which he held.

Piper was the only one who also held a hand of cards.

Most of the chips by now were divided between Piper and Emmet.

Emmet glanced at Piper's face which remained immobile. It was like a heathen black idol's, Emmet thought.

The others waited.

Emmet laid down his cards.

"Two couples," he said. "Jack high."

It was Piper's turn. He laid down his cards.

"Sorry," he said and raked in the pot.

Mrs. Hacker swept up the deck. She sorted the cards, shuffled them and dealt another round. Her movements were expert and deft.

Emmet looked around the table. He was still smiling amiably, even though he had lost the last hand to Piper. He lifted his glass.

"Is there another bottle on the premises, Mr. Hacker?" he asked.

Hacker said mildly, "Ground rules, Mr. Emmet. One bottle on card nights," he reminded him. "Since you're new to the game, we—"

"Nothing to be afraid of, Mr. Hacker!" Emmet put in. "I don't get drunk." He said it in his most affable manner.

"Oh, it's not that," Hacker assured him with his air of courtly reserve. "It's just that we like to think of Tuesday night as a night for playing cards, not carousing."

"Can't change the rule to two bottles?" Emmet grinned. "Just for tonight?"

O'Hara turned to the chauffeur. "We try to keep Tuesday night convivial, Mr. Emmet," he pronounced solemnly. "Just a nice, convivial night."

"I'll take two, Mrs. Hacker," Piper said.

She tossed him two cards.

"Two, please," O'Hara said.

"Three, thank you," said Hacker.

Brian came down the backstairs into the kitchen at that

moment. No one bothered to get up. The players, their eyes fastened on their cards, murmured perfunctory greetings. Brian pulled up a chair behind Mrs. Hacker.

Emmet shifted his cigar to the other side of his mouth.

"I'll take one," he told Mrs. Hacker, "if you make it an ace!"

"Dealer—one," said Mrs. Hacker.

Hacker raised his eyes from the perusal of his hand.

"Mr. Emmet," he remarked, "have you met Mrs. Hacker's nephew, Brian Mallory?"

"Emmet, is it?" Brian said. "How do you do, Mr. Emmet."

Emmet glanced at him. "How are you, Brian?" he said cordially. Then his eyes shifted back to his cards.

"The game," Mrs. Hacker remarked to Brian, "is called poker."

"I know it well," he told her with a rueful look.

Piper tossed his chips into the center of the table.

"Ten, twenty, thirty, forty, *fifty* cents," he proclaimed.

O'Hara and Hacker in turn tossed their chips onto the pile.

They turned to Emmet. It was his turn.

"Well," he said, "I suppose it's time to make this cheesy game a little interesting." He flung a handful of chips onto the cloth. "Fifty cents," he declared. "And I raise you five dollars."

"Sorry, Mr. Emmet," Hacker said quietly. "The rules say—"

"Ah, now, Hacker," Emmet cried. "Let's play for a little blood!"

"It's only a convivial game, Mr. Emmet," O'Hara protested. "Nobody's supposed to lose his shirt."

"I'm in the hole eleven bucks," Emmet informed him. He picked up his glass and drained it. Then he set it down with a loud laugh. "That adds up to four shirts!" he said.

Mrs. Hacker said with decision, "Can we finish the hand? And," she added, "shall we say that it's the last hand? It's getting late, you know."

The regulars nodded.

"Aye," said O'Hara.

"Good idea," Piper chimed in.

"The ayes have it," Hacker concluded. He pushed Emmet's chips back to the chauffeur. "Would you care to make that bet over again, Mr. Emmet?"

Emmet turned his most amiable smile on Hacker.

"You got an arrangement with the wife here?" he said. "She calls it quits when you're ahead?"

Very deliberately, Hacker laid down his hand. He was about to reply when Brian spoke up.

"That's not a friendly thing to say," he said.

Emmet turned slowly and faced Brian. When he addressed him it was without the slightest trace of rancor in his voice. There was even a smile on his lips.

"Sonny," he observed, "the place is lousy enough with her nieces. I don't want to hear from any nephews."

"Sir," Brian began.

Emmet turned to Hacker. Still smiling, and in a tone of absolute agreeableness, he inquried, "Is that all she *can* give birth to? Nieces and nephews?"

Mrs. Hacker's face went pale. The others sat there in shocked silence.

Hacker was the first to recover.

"Mister Emmet!" he said, very quietly and with dignity.

Emmet gave him a commiserating smile.

"You poor bastard," he remarked. "Playing papa to nothing but nieces and nephews and canaries!"

Mrs. Hacker hurriedly left the room. They could hear her footsteps rushing up the backstairs.

Emmet looked around him.

"Something wrong?" he inquired. "Did I say something wrong?"

Hacker stood up.

Brian quickly got to his feet and inserted his body between Hacker and Emmet. Emmet remained seated.

"Sir!" Brian cried. "You are a loudmouthed pig."

Emmet regarded him calmly.

"Would you care to step outside and say that again?" he demanded.

"Delighted," Brian told him. "But before I do, it is only fair and decent to tell you that I have been, for three consecutive years, the amateur welterweight champion of the British Isles." He stood there like a fighting bantam cock and glared at the chauffeur. "Are you still of a mind to step outside with me?"

Emmet rose, very slowly, staring fixedly at Brian. Then he sent his fist crashing into Brian's belly.

Brian doubled over and dropped to the floor where he sprawled, groaning.

Without giving him another glance, Harry Emmet picked up his coat from the back of the chair and left the room.

Brian opened his eyes again to see the concerned faces of Piper and O'Hara bending over him.

"The British Isles," O'Hara was pronouncing in his most solemn tones, "include England, Ireland, Scotland and Wales. Do they not?"

"True," Brian managed to gasp.

Piper regarded him open-mouthed.

"And you was *champeen*?" he demanded.

"In a manner of speaking," Brian admitted faintly.

"What manner of speaking, Mr. Mallory?" O'Hara inquired.

Brian flushed. He waited for a spasm of pain to pass before he answered.

"I have never claimed any proficiency as a pugilist," he said at last. "I was champion welterweight liar of England, Ireland, Scotland and Wales. Champion *liar*, Mr.

O'Hara." Slowly he raised his head and looked around. "Uncle—" he called.

There was no answer.

Mr. Hacker was nowhere in sight.

CHAPTER NINETEEN: COMPARATIVE POLITICS

Hacker had wasted no time in going upstairs and seeing to Mrs. Hacker.

He found her in their bedroom, stretched out on their big brass double bed. She was in tears.

He sat down beside her. He took her hand, pressed it and held it. He waited until her tears stopped flowing. Then he took his handkerchief and dabbed her eyes.

"Give it to me," she said.

He handed her the handkerchief.

She mopped her face with it and scrubbed her cheeks.

"There," he said. "Do you feel any better now?"

She shook her head.

"The man is stupid," he said. "Worse. He is a fool."

Mrs. Hacker bit her lips and fought back another rush of tears. "To say a thing like that—"

"It was a drunken and foolish thing to say," Hacker admitted.

"And in front of the others!"

"My dear," he reassured her, "the others are your friends."

They were interrupted by someone knocking on the door.

"I don't want to see anybody!"

Hacker kissed her gently. "You have retired for the evening," he told her. He turned off the overhead light and stepped through the bead portieres into their parlor, closing the seldom-used door behind him.

The canaries had stopped chirping, all their cages shrouded for the night.

When he opened the door he found Brian standing in the hallway.

"Is she all right?" Brian asked.

"Come in," Hacker told him softly.

Then, as Brian stepped inside and he could see the boy's face, he added, "Are *you* all right?"

"I'm standing up," Brian replied.

All the same, Hacker thought, the boy's face looked queer. It had a decidedly greenish cast to it.

He gestured to Brian to sit down. Then he went to the sideboard and poured two generous drinks.

"What makes him so mean?" Brian demanded.

"He was drunk," Hacker said.

"You're sure of that?"

Hacker turned and looked sharply at him. This was a thought which had not occurred to him.

"You'll fire him, I take it," Brian said.

"No," Hacker replied. "That's not within my authority."

"Why not?" Brian insisted.

"Mr. Emmet is directly responsible to Mr. Lassiter," Hacker answered. "Not to me."

"But if he's only the chauffeur—"

"He's a little more than that," Hacker replied.

"What's a little more than that?"

Hacker handed Brian his drink and lowered himself heavily into a chair to face him.

"Well," Hacker explained in his quiet, reasonable voice, "as far as I can make out, Emmet also does some confidential work for Mr. Lassiter."

"Confidential?" Brian echoed, frowning. "What does Lassiter need a confidential agent for?"

"Mr. Lassiter," Hacker explained with a shrug, pointedly emphasizing the word *mister* for Brian's benefit, "is in politics." He jerked his thumb at the glass in Brian's hand. "Here," he said. "You'd better drink some of that. You need it. You never know when you'll have a chance to win back your championship title."

Brian took a long gulp of his drink. It set him coughing. When he had recovered he returned to the subject of Emmet, like a dog worrying a bone.

"Well," he said, "why don't you tell *Mr.* Lassiter what the bastard just did? Tell him what sort of a mean little bastard—"

Hacker cut him short.

"I couldn't do that, Brian," he said.

"Why not?"

"Well, for one thing, it's a matter of comparative politics."

"Comparative politics?"

Hacker nodded.

"I never heard of that,'" Brian said.

"There's a lot you never heard of back in Ireland," Hacker reminded him.

"Anyway," Brian demanded belligerently, "now that I've heard of it, what does it mean?"

Hacker took a slow, appreciative sip of his drink.

"It means," he said, "that the petty politics of life back here must never intrude in the politics of *their* lives." He paused and fixed Brian with his eyes. "And I'll thank you to remember that."

"All right," Brian conceded. "If that's how you feel.

But," he went on, "d'you suppose it's smart of Mr. Lassiter to put his confidence in a loudmouth like that?"

"No," admitted Hacker. "I do not."

"And wouldn't it be all to Mr. Lassiter's benefit to be relieved of the services of such a brute?" he demanded.

For a long time Hacker sat there studying the boy, without speaking.

Finally he held up his glass.

Brian raised his.

They drank thoughtfully, in silence.

CHAPTER TWENTY: A WAITING CAR ON PINCKNEY STREET

At the bottom of Pinckney Street a convertible coupé stood parked beside the curb, as far as possible from the street lamp.

It was late at night. The car had been waiting there for almost an hour. It had its flaps up, concealing the occupant from the curious stare of anyone who might be passing by. At that hour, however, it was not likely that residents of Beacon Hill would be out walking on the streets.

Betsy Bullock sat at the wheel of the car, huddled inside her thick coat and peering through the windshield into the night. She was anxious and impatient. She glanced at her watch to verify the time ten times in as many minutes. Then each time she would squint out at the dark street.

And each time it was only to ascertain once again that Pinckney Street, from the Charles River to Louisburg Square, was deserted.

She had almost given up hope when she heard the footsteps approaching on the street outside.

Was it—? She almost dreaded to look. And then, when she saw that it was, after all, the one person she had been waiting for, the anxiety drained out of her soft young face. Relief and joy illuminated it.

Quickly she leaned over to the passenger side and opened the door.

A dark figure slid into the car beside her, slamming the door shut behind him. Wordlessly, he took her into his arms.

She was tremulous now and almost in tears as she pressed her lips against his mouth. She held herself against him.

Then, after a while, she pulled her mouth away from his and rested her cheek against his. She liked the rough texture of his shaven face, the smell of him: a thrilling mixture of heavy tobacco and Florida water and the damp wool of his coat.

"I've been waiting and waiting," she cried. "I thought I'd die if you didn't come!"

She stared into his face looking for confirmation of her quivering joy in his actual presence, waiting for a word of apology, of explanation, of—she wasn't sure what it was she hoped for!

"I told you I'd be late," Emmet said, brusquely.

Had she done something wrong? Should she have seemed less eager? He couldn't be worried that someone had seen her there. There was no one to see her! Why did he seem so—so sullen?

"Where *were* you?" she demanded. "I've been waiting here since—"

"Had some business with grandpa," he told her. "Where else could I have been?"

She ran her finger along the hard line of his jaw.

"At this time of night?" she asked.

"That's the job, sweetheart," he said. "I'm on tap twenty-four hours a day. When he calls, I come."

"Do you always drink when you confer with my grandfather?" Betsy said.

"Why?"

She made a face. "You smell like a saloon," she said.

He drew his face impatiently away from her exploring finger.

"You know that there's always a bottle in the old man's room," he said. "You know that."

She eyed him adoringly. She loved the way Emmet looked, sulky, ruthless, unpredictable and moody. It wasn't his fault that Emmet was only a chauffeur. If the world weren't so upside down and so unfair, he'd be—well, something quite marvelous and commanding.

"I think he takes advantage of you," she declared, looking thoughtful and solicitous.

"Could be," Emmet admitted.

"Well," she said. "He's wasted enough of our time." She leaned forward, her fingers on the ignition key.

Emmet put his hand over hers, preventing her from turning on the motor.

"Sweetheart," he said.

She looked at him and frowned.

"What's the matter?"

He shook his head. "I can't," he said. "Not tonight."

"What?"

"I'm sorry."

"Why not?"

"You can guess," he said glumly.

She slumped back in the seat and stared through the isinglass windows of the car flaps at the shadowy street.

"More of grandpa's business!" she exclaimed.

"That's right," Emmet said. "I've got to get back as soon as I can."

"But, but that's simply hateful!" she stormed.

Emmet shrugged again.

"It's not my fault," he reminded her.

"It *is* your fault!" she insisted. "You know that!"

Instead of replying, he pulled her toward him and covered her pouting mouth with his. But this time, instead of yielding, she writhed out of his embrace.

"I insist that we go to your place right now," she told him imperiously. "I don't care who—"

"That's enough," he told her. "Now keep quiet."

She gasped. She stared at him with blazing hostility in her eyes. How dared Harry tell her to keep quiet!

He merely smiled grimly at her until she was compelled to lower her gaze.

"Harry," she pleaded. "Ple-e-e-ease!"

"Tomorrow night, sweetheart," he said.

He opened the door and got out. Then he leaned in.

"Maybe," he added.

He slammed the door shut. And then he was gone. All she could see was his dark broad back as he strode up Pinckney Street.

"Harry!" she called after him. But he had not heard, or, if he had, he gave no sign of it.

Betsy sat there at the wheel, not doing anything to stop the tears that ran down her soft, young, puppyish and willful face.

CHAPTER TWENTY-ONE: HORTENSE'S HOUSE

Hortense's house was a quiet, well-cared-for brownstone on an otherwise dingy street in a rundown section of the city. It was in a part of Boston which, before the war, had been respectable and uncompromisingly lower middle class. In the past few years its aspect had subtly changed. The crisp lace curtains at the windows, washed and stretched once a month by respectable Irish housewives, had by now almost all been replaced by gaudier hangings behind which could be seen black faces.

It was just an ordinary night at Hortense's when Emmet got there and was admitted by a black maid in a dark uniform and a big organdy bow in her hair. He stood just inside the doorway for a moment, looking around at the Victorian parlor with its heavy dark-stained woodwork and its lamps with their big pleated georgette shades. Hortense always kept the lights low, glowing pinkly in the room. There was an upright piano in a corner where a black pianist played ragtime. There were a few white customers sitting around at the tables, talking to the girls. A few couples were on the floor, dancing. There was a long bar with a black man tending it.

The Lassiter family of Louisburg Square. Seated (l. to r.): Mary Lassiter (Nancy Marchand), Betsy Bullock (Linda Purl), Benjamin Lassiter (Stephen Elliott). Standing (l. to r.): Robert Lassiter (David Dukes), Rosamond Lassiter (Kitty Winn), Fawn Lassiter (Kathryn Walker), Maude Lassiter Palmer (Maeve McGuire), Richard Palmer (Edward Hermann), Emily Lassiter Bullock (DeAnn Mears), Trevor Bullock (Roy Cooper).

Benjamin Lassiter, returning from Europe, arrives at his Beacon Hill mansion on the eve of Prohibition.

Yachtsman Richard Palmer corners his father-in-law, wife Maude (far left), and her sister Emily

Mary Lassiter, on chaise longue, plans Prohibition party with secretary Marilyn Gardner (Holland Taylor), left, and housekeeper Emmeline Hacker (Beatrice Straight).

Mrs. Hacker presents her nephew, Brian Mallory (Paul Rudd).

Mrs. Hacker prepares to deal to (l. to r.): William Piper (Richard Ward), Terence O'Hara (David Rounds), Harry Emmet (Barry Snider), and her husband, Arthur Hacker (George Rose).

The staff belowstairs. Mrs. Hacker sits before (l. to r.) Mr. Hacker, Terence O'Hara, Kate (Lisa Pelikan), Eleanor, (Sydney Swire), Maureen (Susan Blanchard), William Piper, and Brian Mallory.

William Piper, watched by Brian, prepares the multi-course dinner for the Lassiters and guests.

Under Mrs. Hacker's supervision, Eleanor (far left) and Kate perfect the table setting.

Mr. and Mrs. Lassiter lead their guests into dinner as Mrs. Hacker looks on.

Fawn Lassiter makes an entrance.

Robert Lassiter, customary drink in hand, is assisted into his dinner jacket by Terence O'Hara.

Emily Bullock (right) confronts her daughter Betsy over after dinner coffee. Terence, in background, waits to be of service.

Fawn (right) flirts with brother-in-law Richard Palmer as her sister Maude watches.

Rosamond, youngest of the tour Lassiter sisters, leaves mansion with newly appointed chauffeur, Brian Mallory.

Robert Lassiter, alone in his room.

Hortense liked to say that what she ran was a "house of all nations." But that was just Hortense. True, she did have one girl who looked vaguely Chinese and another who was probably a half-breed, but all the other girls were black—black and handpicked.

Emmet moved forward until he stood at the edge of the dance floor. He ignored all the couples except one. He steadily watched this pair as they moved around the floor. The man was white-haired and elderly, potbellied, with an Elk's tooth dangling from the watch chain stretched across his vest, and the look of a small-time businessman out for a good time. The girl was thin and her skin was a glowing light brown in color. She was laughing as she danced, doing a lithe shimmy.

When they passed Emmet, he yanked the girl from her elderly partner's arms.

"This is my dance, Viola," Emmet said and, to the Elk's annoyance, went stepping off with her.

Viola said, making a show of being angry, "You could be more polite!"

"Come on, Viola!" he told her. "Are you telling me you'd rather have him than me?"

Suddenly their dance was interrupted by a large black hand tapping Emmet on the shoulder. Without bothering to look up to see to whom it belonged, he brushed it aside and moved Viola toward the middle of the floor.

The hand tapped his shoulder again.

He turned this time to face the intruder.

An imperious black woman was facing him. There was no telling what her age might be, probably somewhere near forty. She had a shrewd mannish face under her full head of hair, which was pulled down over her mahogany cheeks in French dips. Her long gown was black lace with an organdy rose at her belt. It was remarkably stylish and she knew it. A long cascade of pearls fell over her massive bust. At her side stood the white-haired man, fuming with outrage, like a bullied schoolboy who had run to get help.

"You drunk?" the woman demanded, casting a quick, appraising eye over Emmet.

"Drunk?" he echoed. "I'm just happy, Hortense. J-u-u-u-ust happy!"

She fixed the girl with a hard glance.

"Viola," she commanded, "you go and finish your dance with Mr. Carpenter."

"Sure!" the girl said.

With a look of haughty disdain, Viola disengaged herself from Emmet's grip and shimmied off in the elderly man's arms.

Hortense watched them move off. Then she crooked a finger at Emmet and moved across the dance floor like a galleon in full sail.

Emmet trailed jauntily in her wake.

Behind the bar hung a pair of heavy plush curtains. Hortense pushed them aside, rattling their wooden rungs. Behind them was revealed a small, highly varnished door with a small pane of glass set in it at eye level. She opened it now and nodded to him to follow her inside.

Hortense's private parlor was small and neat, furnished with an overstuffed suite consisting of a sofa and two chairs upholstered in figured red velvet. A standing lamp stood behind the sofa, crowned with a vast shade of fringed rose satin, trimmed with a swag of satin fruit.

"Like it?" she said.

"Not bad," he admitted.

Hortense set her rhinestone-studded comb more securely into her back hair. "I did it up myself," she said.

She gestured him to a chair and sailed across to a brightly japanned sideboard.

"What's makin' you happy?" she asked. "Scotch?"

He nodded. "Scotch'll do," he said.

She poured him a drink. "I'm sorry I had to talk to you

that way. But I gotta keep Mr. Carpenter happy. I don't know why it is, but white gentlemen always get so—well, touchy, when they mix their colors. It's like mixing drinks. You understand."

"It's okay," Emmet said.

She handed him his drink. Then she sat down, facing him.

"What's on your mind?" Emmet asked her.

She adjusted, unnecessarily, the clutch of organdy roses at her waist. Then she said, "I got a problem."

"You callin' on me to fix a problem?" Emmet said, giving an imitation of her accent. "I'm mighty flattered, Miss Hortense."

She brushed aside his vaudeville voice, indicating with a brief, majestic gesture that she had no time for such nonsense right now.

"Listen," she said.

"I'm listening," he told her.

"You never did know Floyd Prince, did you?"

"No," he replied. "And who the hell is he?"

"Floyd Prince is the gentleman who had this idea in the first place. Floyd left this house to me when he died because he loved me, and I loved him. He left me with the establishment, that was what he always called it, and the reputation and the clientele: nice, respectable white gentlemen who knew that they'd get treated fair and square—no panel games, no blackmail, no low tricks. And Floyd left me the boss. I never changed the policy. I did put in the music, but I never changed the policy." She glanced over toward him sharply. "You followin' me?"

Emmet nodded. "Yes," he said. "I'm following you, but I don't know where you're taking me."

"Just give me another minute and we'll get there," she answered. "I'm tellin' you all this because you bring me a lot of trade and I don't want to hurt your feelings."

"Oh," he countered. "So you're going to hurt my feelings now . . ."

"No! I'm saying that I don't want to do that." She held up a heavy square hand. "Now hold on," she said. "Let me talk. For sixteen years I been running this establishment on an A-number-one policy. I only serve bonded liquor. There's real carpets on the floor, no sawdust. Hand crocheted doilies on all the furniture. *Nice* pictures on the walls—no naked hussies showing what they got and what they ain't got. I got my saloon license and I got my arrangements with the boys over at the precinct. I never make no trouble and they never give me no trouble." She paused and eyed him. "You still following me?"

"Yeah. But I still can't figure out what it's all leading up to."

"So on Friday night, midnight," she said, "all that's going right out the window."

"Yeah," he said. "I read the newspapers. I heard about it, Hortense."

"Well," she said, pushing back her heavy shoulders and drawing herself up, "I got to tell you right off—Miss Hortense is not closing up here."

He smiled, cocking his head to one side. "You're not?"

"No, sir," she said with quiet vehemence. "Miss Hortense is going to go right on, running this establishment with the same old policy, providing a little ease, a little comfort and relaxation for her white customers. Sure, I got to do it without the license, but I already made my arrangements with the boys over at the precinct. They're not going to close me down till we all get a good look at how this Prohibition thing's going to work—if it is going to work. Grace time, that's what we all calling it. Two weeks grace, and see if we can stay open without them federal cops and all jumping on us and closing us down. We going to see if decent honest people can run a nice clean dry business even if Lily Law says "No!" It's going to be a whole new world. And the trick of licking it, I'm here to tell you right now, is to stay away from trouble. No trouble, no how. You still following me?"

Emmet nodded.

"I'm with you so far, Miss Hortense," he told her.

"The least noise in here," she went on, "the least little step out of line, the precinct boys say they're going to close me down. Arrangement or no arrangement. They got a right to be nice to me because they got a lot of my good greenbacks in their time, and a lot of free rides on the house, if you get my meaning. But that was when I was operating about fifty per cent inside the law. But now it's going to be operating one hundred per cent *outside* the law, and I got to walk a very, very, very straight line. No slipping. And no trouble! Not a speck of it." She paused and regarded him steadily while he finished his drink.

When he put his empty glass down, she said, "You ready now?"

"I'm ready," he said.

"All right. You come to take him home, you take him."

He looked at her, puzzled.

"Is that supposed to hurt my feelings?" he asked.

"No," she said. "Not yet. I ain't said it yet."

"Well," he told her, "say it."

"Okay." She leaned forward, propping up her weight with her hands on her massive knees. "Don't never bring him back," she said.

He gaped at her.

"What?"

Her voice rose. "Why didn't you ever tell me who he was?" she demanded. "I didn't know who he was! I had no *idea* who he was!" She let out a long, scornful hoot. "Mr. Brown! In a pig's eye, Mr. Brown!" she said.

For a long moment Emmet regarded her in silence.

"All right," he said finally. "You tell me. Who is he?"

She slapped her thigh with the flat of her hand. "I don't

want no Lassiters in here!" she said. "Not from now on, I don't."

His eyes narrowed.

"How did you find out?" he demanded.

"There's nothing that goes on in Miss Hortense's house that she doesn't find out about, sooner or later," she said.

"How did you find out?" he repeated.

She considered another evasive reply, then dismissed the idea.

"All right," she said. "I'll tell you the truth. That's the kind of establishment I run here. That new girl who went with him tonight, she went through his wallet. I whupped her good for that. And don't worry, nobody took no money. But she seen his name. And—"

"And what?"

"And," she declared flatly, "I don't want no Lassiters in here."

"Why not?" he asked, smiling up at her. "It might do you some good."

"Are you crazy?" she told him. "Don't you read the papers like you say you do? Friday night they going to have a million cops all over this city, coming up to examine everybody, and they going to be all over us from then on. You know what'll happen after Friday when somebody like that gets caught in here? I get *my* name in the papers, which is one place it's never been. And poom!" She punched the fist of one hand into the palm of the other, making a loud smacking sound. "There goes my good business."

Emmet said, "You sure, now?"

"Sure I'm sure. I wouldn't waste all this breath if I wasn't. Just get him out of here for good and all! Please do that little thing for Miss Hortense!"

Emmet got up.

He drew out his wallet and sent several bills floating

down into her lap. Then he started wordlessly for the door.

"Mr. Smith!" Hortense called after him.

"Yeah?" He half-turned toward her.

"That don't mean *you* can't come back," she said.

He laughed.

"I'll remember that, Hortense," he said.

He went out then.

CHAPTER TWENTY-TWO: BOBBY BOY

Emmet made his way upstairs. He knew where to go, and which door to open.

The room was dimly lit by a small beaded bedside lamp. The thick curtains were drawn. The air was heavy with the smell of whisky and a musky, pervasive perfume.

He walked over to the foot of the bed and looked down at its single occupant. In the stillness he could hear the heavy sleeper's heavy breathing. He waited, but the sleeper did not stir.

Emmet then stepped around to the side of the bed and sat down on the edge of it. He leaned over and peered at Robert Lassiter. Robert's head was buried in the pillow. His shoulders were naked.

"Mr. Robert—" Emmet said in a low voice.

There was no response.

Emmet reached for Robert's chin and roughly shook him.

"Time to get dressed," he said. "Time to go home." He grabbed Robert by his good arm and hauled him into a sitting position. "Come on, Bobby Boy," Emmet said. Emmet was no longer smiling.

CHAPTER TWENTY-THREE: A SINGING LESSON

Fawn Lassiter's Back Bay "studio," as she called it, was an apartment at the top of an old building. She liked its high ceiling and the skylight in the living room because, she claimed, it gave her a sense of the "freedom necessary for her being!"

And, from her surroundings, it was evident that Fawn's being required a great deal of freedom.

There were vast, unfinished canvases on the walls. The furniture was an undigested mixture of heavy Renaissance pieces mingled with nondescript chairs and tables which Fawn had picked up here and there and painted in bright colors. There were vivid cushions thrown about everywhere. The general effect was that of the Russian ballet into which a set from a Schubert operetta had somehow intruded.

It was, however, as Fawn told everyone who came to see her, the effect which counted, and the effect was thoroughly satisfying to her. She felt that it was properly Bohemian, as befitted a free soul, an artistic spirit. For Fawn Lassiter was, above all things, dedicated to the arts.

The art she was engaged in on this January afternoon was that of music. She was having a singing lesson.

She stood beside the splendid black Steinway grand which filled the center of the room, her pretty mouth open wide in song. Her hair fell loosely around her shoulders, and she wore a long peacock-colored peignoir with voluminous georgette sleeves.

" 'Un bel' di vedremo . . .'," Fawn sang, and Puccini's music emerged sweet and clear and poignant from her throat. Fawn's voice, while not perhaps of concert quality, was a pleasant one.

A dark-haired young man in shirt sleeves sat on the piano bench, performing her accompaniment. Suddenly, in mid-aria, he hit a crashing chord and stopped playing.

Fawn broke off, reacting as though she had been slapped.

"What now, for heaven's sakes?" she shouted.

"I tell you again and again and again!" the young man shouted back, in a heavy Italian accent. He ran his hands through his glossy hair. "On the arpeggio you step very lightly. You do not, how do you say? kick it!"

"I'm terribly sorry," Fawn said with carefully enunciated hauteur.

"Do not be *angry* with me!" he pleaded.

"Start again, please, Maestro," she answered, staring at the curtained skylight implacably. She tapped her bare foot in its brocaded mule. "I am waiting for you to begin, *caro* Maestro Giorgio Bellonci!"

"Fawn!" he warned. "Do not be temperamental with *me!* You are not yet a prima donna!"

"Strike your chord, Maestro!"

Giorgio Bellonci sighed in exasperation. Then he rose from the piano bench and moved close to her. She raised her chin and stared defiantly into his face. He seized her by the shoulders and pulled her toward him. When he kissed her she offered no cooperation. She merely permitted herself to be kissed.

Bellonci drew back and shook his head.

"This," he said, "is what comes of taking a lesson after making love." He look his head again. "It is against the nature," he pronounced.

He stood there, regarding her forlornly.

Fawn studied him. Then she threw back her head and broke into loud laughter. "Poor Butterfly!" she cried. "Anyway, I've had enough of her for one day." She wound her arms around him cajolingly. This time, the kiss was one in which they were both involved.

A loud ringing of the doorbell interrupted it.

Fawn jerked her mouth away from Bellonci's.

Giorgio said in an alarmed whisper, to Fawn, "Who is it?"

"How do I know?" she whispered back. Then she shouted, "Who is it?"

"Fawn?" called a man's voice from the other side of the door.

Fawn clapped her hand to her mouth.

"Oh, my God!" she exclaimed.

Giorgio's alarm visibly increased.

"Who is it?" he repeated in an even lower whisper.

"There's no time to get dressed," she whispered back. She pushed him toward the bedroom door. "Lock the door!" she ordered. "Just stay in there! Don't come out!"

"I do not understand—" Giorgio began, his handsome face sagging in sullen bewilderment. Suddenly he no longer looked quite so young as he had.

Fawn thrust him inside the bedroom, making sure that the door was firmly shut behind him. She ran her hands nervously over her peignoir and made a quick stab at arranging her hair—there were some hairpins on the piano. She rubbed her face with her fingers.

She was ready now.

Fawn had always had a gift for sudden control. Improvisation in the face of turbulence had been, since her childhood, a useful talent. Now she took a deep breath, stiffened her back and with composed, elegant strides advanced to the door of the studio. She flung it open and stood there within the frame, her arms stretched out in what had every appearance of being a spontaneous gesture of welcome.

Benjamin Lassiter was standing there, impatiently waiting to be admitted.

She flung her arms around him. "Daddy!" she cried, clinging to him.

"We've been home three days," he remarked when he had untangled himself.

"I know," she said.

She led him into the room. She took his hat from his hand. "Give me your overcoat, Daddy," she said and helped him out of it.

"I don't know why you always keep this place so overheated," he observed.

"I'm an orchid, Daddy. Anyway, you raised me like one."

"Where do you want me to sit?"

"Oh, anywhere. It's so good to see you, Daddy!"

He lowered himself onto a couch over which an embroidered Spanish shawl had been draped with artful carelessness. Fawn fussed with the neckline of her peignoir. It was really maddening, she thought, his arriving this way without a moment's warning. She waited for him to say something disapproving about her being dressed, or, rather, undressed in this fashion at such an inappropriate hour, but if he had noticed he said nothing about it.

"Emily came over yesterday with the kids," he informed her.

"I did call, Daddy," she protested.

He cast her a wry glance.

"You figure a telephone conversation is good enough after we've been away for six weeks?"

"Oh, Daddy, I've no excuse. I've been busy, that's all."

He stretched out his legs, which ended in clocked black silk socks and hand-sewn London shoes.

"How's the career going?" he asked.

"Just plain bloody godawful," she answered, putting on a glum face.

"What's the matter?" he asked. "What's gone wrong this time?"

"Oh," she said. She tossed her head petulantly. "With my looks, and my talent, and my voice, I just seem to be getting nowhere."

"Perhaps," he observed drily, "if you weren't so modest—"

She swooped over to him and planted a quick kiss on his forehead.

"I have a new teacher," she announced.

"Ah," he said. "A good one?"

"I think that he's absolutely marvelous, but—" She broke off and began roaming around the room, picking up bibelots and restlessly putting them down again. She ended up pacing back and forth in front of the bedroom door, twisting her long fingers in her shiny hair as she talked.

"Oh, Daddy!" she exclaimed. "I've been having such violent thoughts."

"What?" he put in. "In that outfit? No wonder you keep this place so overheated."

"Do be serious, Daddy," she pouted. "You never were with me. That's the whole trouble. Listen. I've been thinking very seriously of going to Europe."

"Why not New York? That's nearer, and it's just as foreign," he suggested.

She shook her head. "It has to be Europe for a singer," she reminded him.

"Where? Paris?"

"Paris? Pooh. Paris is no place for a voice, Daddy. The opera there is a complete mess. Unless," she added contemptuously, "all you care about is Mayerbeer and Massenet."

"Massenet is good enough for Mary Garden," he reminded her.

"Mary Garden! I'm going to be better, lots better, Daddy. I was thinking of Milano, maybe. Some place where there's still respect for real singing, where the *bel canto* tradition is still alive. I'll start all over again. I might even take a new name. What do you think?"

"What's wrong with your name?"

"That name! Whatever possessed you to let mother name me Fawn!"

"Fawn, you know perfectly well that Maude and Emily were named after your grandmothers. When you came along we'd run out of grandmothers, and there was this character in a novel that your mother had been reading. I like it. Fawn. It's pretty."

"Yes," she sneered. "And who ever heard of a serious singer with a name like Fawn Lassiter? I was thinking I'd have to find something more appropriate."

"Like what?"

"Like, well, Vanna di Lasso. How does that strike you?"

He laughed. "It's a strike all right," he said.

"I'm serious!" she stormed at him. "Daddy, you don't seem to realize that I'm despondent!"

"The hell with singing," he said.

"Daddy!"

"Why don't you go into the movies and show them how to act. It's one thing you can do without taking any lessons. You take that Theda Bara—"

"Theda Bara!" she repeated contemptuously. "That silly old vamp!"

"She's managed to vamp her way to the bank with a couple of cool millions," he told her. "What's the new teacher like?" he asked.

"I told you. Absolutely marvelous!"

"Is he the one who's hiding in the bedroom?"

She suddenly stopped pacing and glared at him. She opened her mouth to raise a vehement denial, but before she could speak he waggled his finger in the air at her.

She suddenly adopted a little girl's voice.

"How did you know?" she giggled.

"Easy," he said. "You're not talking to me. You've been saying it all to that door."

"All right," she admitted, pouting in defeat. "You win. You always do, Daddy."

"And you're always up to some mischief," he said.

"I like mischief. It amuses me!" she confessed. Then, on an impulse of perverse delight, she went to the door and flung it open. It was a gesture straight out of La Tosca.

There was a long moment of static silence.

And then, slowly, from the bedroom emerged not Scarpia, but Giorgio Bellonci, shamefaced and ruffled, nervously trying to attach his collar to his shirt.

"Father," announced Fawn, "this is Giorgio Bellonci!"

"Hello, Giorgio," Benjamin Lassiter said, easily, not bothering to rise from the fringes of the Spanish shawl.

"Mr. Lassiter, sir," said Giorgio, flustered.

Benjamin glanced from one to the other—Giorgio in his shirt sleeves, Fawn in her negligée.

"I wouldn't want to jump to any rash conclusions," he said judiciously. "But this air of"—he cleared his throat—"of general informality. Am I wrong in assuming that you two are very good friends?"

Giorgio cleared his throat in turn.

"Well, sir," he began.

"The *best* of friends, Daddy," Fawn said.

"Thank you, Fawn. Do we offend you, Giorgio, by getting right to the point in our crude American way?"

"Frankly, sir, I am very, ah—" He stared at the ceiling, as though the word he were searching for might be written there.

Fawn supplied it.

"Bewildered," she said.

Benjamin Lassiter leaned back expansively. "Oh, now, relax," he said. "Nobody's going to bite. Giorgio, I do not sit in judgment on the private lives of my children." He considered briefly. "No," he said. "I'll qualify that. I do sit in judgment but I never hand down any verdicts. I think that Fawn, for instance, makes herself very unhappy trying out all these startling new methods of being happy. She wants to be modern. For some reason it's important to her. Personally, I think that she wastes a lot of energy trying to shock herself. No, Fawn," he went on, holding up a restraining hand. "Let me finish. What I want to say is that we're long past the stage when I say 'Stop it, or papa spank!' Fawn is a grown woman. She is thirty-three years old."

"Daddy!" Fawn expostulated.

"Oops! Sorry, Fawnie. I meant to say twenty-nine."

She made a face at him. He merely ignored it and turned toward Giorgio.

"Fawn," he informed him, "is what those novelists call 'a free soul.' That gives her the right to paint pictures no one else can figure out, or write poetry that doesn't rhyme, or take singing lessons in her nightgown. That's all right," he conceded. "All poets are entitled to a certain amount of poetic license. Fawnie lives her life without any restrictions imposed by papa. She can make any kind of a damned fool of herself that she wants." He paused and held up his hand. "Up to a point," he added.

Giorgio was staring at Benjamin Lassiter, at the same time appalled and fascinated by what he heard.

"And just what is that point?" Benjamin demanded. "Is that what you're dying to ask me?"

"Yes, sir," Giorgio said, still staring at him.

"It's this," Benjamin declared flatly. "Her mother must never know what kind of a damned fool she is. If she ever embarrasses her mother, I will do what any doting father would do to a wayward daughter." He disentangled himself from the Spanish shawl and got to his feet. He collected his pearl-gray Homburg and his velvet-collared overcoat. He nodded gravely. "I will spank her," he said. He moved lightly and deliberately toward the door. Suddenly he turned. "What are you doing Friday night?" he asked Giorgio.

"Sir?" said Giorgio blankly.

"Come to dinner," Lassiter told him.

"Oh, father!" Fawn cried, clapping her hands. "You give yourself the best exit lines!"

"Ask him to bring you, Fawnie," he said by way of a reply. Then he was out the door and gone.

Giorgio stood there. He seemed paralyzed.

Fawn turned to him, giving him a slow, mischievous, inquiring smile.

Giorgio shook his head. "I think that my English is not so good anymore," he said finally. "I do not understand anything. What did he say?"

CHAPTER TWENTY-FOUR: THE VERY BEST

It was the end of the day. Mary Lassiter was stretched out on the chaise longue in the morning room—now, with the soft lamplight glowing warmly on everything, her evening room.

Close by her Marilyn Gardiner sat with a note pad propped on her knees and a pencil poised above it.

"Can you think of anything else, Mrs. Lassiter?" Marilyn asked.

"I don't think so. You remembered to invite the Brodericks?"

"Yes, Mrs. Lassiter. They're coming. Mrs. Broderick was especially delighted."

"That doesn't surprise me," she said. "Now. I want chrysanthemums for the table. The rest of the house is up to Mr. Faber. I can always rely on him."

"As a matter of fact," Marilyn told her, "he's already suggested chrysanthemums for the table. And he'd like to know what you think of yellow roses in the entrance hall and on the piano."

"That's up to him," Mary said. "I don't really— Hello, darling!' she called.

Benjamin had come into the room. He carried a drink in his hand.

Marilyn hastily rose.

"Am I interrupting anything?" Benjamin asked.

"No, no," Mary reassured him. "Miss Gardiner and I are through. Aren't we, dear?"

"Yes, Mrs. Lassiter."

Marilyn was already at the door.

She smiled at Benjamin.

"Good evening, sir," she said.

"Have a nice evening, Miss Gardiner," he told her.

She nodded. The door closed quietly behind her.

Benjamin leaned over his wife then and kissed her. It was not a perfunctory kiss. Despite the fact that they had been married for nearly forty years, they still enjoyed being together. And Mary still enjoyed his kisses.

"Now sit down and talk to me," she said.

Benjamin pulled up a chair and sat down on it with a sigh.

"Do you think she ever does?" he asked.

"Who ever does what?" she asked.

"Miss Gardiner," he said. "Have a nice evening."

She laughed. "Don't be mean," she said. "It's time for you to tell me what a hard day you've had at the office."

He frowned slightly. "Well," he said, "the Third District *is* one hundred and sixty registrations short."

She was instantly alert. "Christy's fault?" she demanded.

"Who else?"

"You'd better send Gavigan down to the Third. Tell him to ring doorbells, talk to the storekeepers. If it's time to change the district leader, Gavigan is the one to smell it out."

He smiled down at her. "Yes, ma'am," he said. "I'll do that."

"Oh, Ben, I'm sorry!" she cried. "Old busybody! I'm still the brickmaker's bossy daughter."

"Keep it up. You've got a better flair for politics than any of us," he said.

"Not really," she protested.

"I mean it," he said. And he obviously did.

She reached out and patted his knee. "Anyway," she assured him, "let Gavigan worry about the Third District. You don't have to. What else?"

"I went to see Fawn today," he announced.

"You did? How is she?"

"She's fine, fine," she said. "Sends her love."

"*Sends* her love!"

"Well, she's been very busy, and—"

"She *is* coming Friday night?" Mary asked. "She can be so unpredictable at times!"

"Unpredictable? Fawn?" Benjamin chuckled. "I think of all our children, Fawnie's the most predictable, in her way. Anyway, don't worry. She'll be here. Maude'll be here. Emily'll be here."

Mary said thoughtfully, "I really don't understand this Friday night celebration at all."

"Well," he told her, "if everybody's going to have one last toot before Prohibition comes in, why not us? And why not all together? The fact of the matter is—"

"Ben!"

"What?"

"I never really trust you when you start a sentence off by saying 'The fact of the matter is.' "

He cast an amused glance at her.

"Whether you trust me or not," he said, "the fact of the matter is that Fawn wanted us for dinner at her place Friday night. Rob invited us to his club. Emily said that she and Trevor wanted us over. So I just put them all together and told everybody to come *here* on Friday night."

"Ben," she warned. "You're improvising! They didn't really—"

"It's the truth," he said. He reached out and took hold of her hand. "Darling," he said, "we do have nice children." He kissed her again. "The very best," he assured her.

"You and your whisky kisses!" she said. She smiled at him. There were tears in her eyes.

CHAPTER TWENTY-FIVE: A FAMILY PARTY

With the exception of Mayor and Mrs. Broderick and the ubiquitous Marvin Malloy, the celebration on Friday night was really a Lassiter family party.

The house on Louisburg Square glowed with lights and with Mr. Faber's floral arrangements. The maids wore their lace-frilled caps, and their aprons likewise were edged with crisply starched lace. Hacker, impeccable and imperturbable, moved among the guests in the living room, serving the drinks, his watchful eye making sure that the maids who circulated with silver trays of food were doing their job properly. Fortunately for them, they were.

It was a full-dress occasion. The long living room seemed suddenly transformed from its customary brown-gravy aspect into a bower of yellow roses and chrysanthemums, among which moved the men in their white ties and the women in long dresses, their hair piled high and their necks and arms and earlobes adorned with their best jewels. Benjamin and Mayor Broderick stood by the fireplace, talking politics, while Rosamond and Betsy Bullock stood nearby, listening respectfully. Marvin Malloy hovered at Benjamin's elbow, full of self-importance at having been invited, but not sufficiently sure of himself on this occasion to contribute to the conversation. Mrs. Broderick, fat and red-faced in her tight corsets and bronze lace, had not stopped talking animatedly from the moment when she had plumped herself down on the sofa beside Mary Lassiter. Mary Lassiter half-listened to her while she made sure out of the corner of her eye that everything was going smoothly.

She looked superb, did Mary Lassiter, knowing too that every now and then Benjamin glanced over appreciatively in her direction. Her new gown, from Lucille in London, suited her. It was of a soft pastel color with a lace bodice arranged in a crosswise drape, and long lace sleeves falling over her elbow-length white gloves. A satin sash was arranged in an elaborate bow at her left hip. The only jewelry she wore, in contrast to Mrs. Broderick who had adorned herself with virtually everything she owned for the occasion, was a long strand of pearls, descending to her waist, a pair of handsome earrings, each containing a pear-shaped pearl, and a watch set in platinum and diamonds which she wore pinned to the lace at her breast. She may have been born a brickmaker's daughter, Benjamin thought, bursting with pride, but his Mary looked, as the saying went, every inch a real lady. There wasn't a single one of those old Boston families that could boast of someone with Mary Lassiter's look of quiet class.

In another part of the room the husbands of the two married Lassiter girls faced each other. Trevor Bullock, was in comparison to the Lassiters, old Boston and old money. He was a handsome, balding, heavy-set man. Everything about him—his face, his clothes, his manner, his voice—bore the hallmark of good breeding, good schools, good food—and social solidity behind it all. At the moment, however, he was being monumentally bored by his brother-in-law, although he did his best not to reveal it.

As usual, Richard Palmer was going on animatedly about sailing.

Their wives, meanwhile, sat side by side on a sofa, thoroughly conscious of the effect they were creating. They were, as always, a spectacular pair of sisters. On this particular evening they had both taken pains to look their best. Maude was enveloped in a celadon chiffon cloud, around a very low-cut beaded gown, to which Emily's saffron evening dress formed a striking contrast. Emily was thoroughly aware of the fact, however, that Maude had worn the same dress last year, while her own was being revealed for the first time, having just been sent up from New York. This, nevertheless, did not quite make up for the fact that Maude's jewels were better than hers. She would have to say something to Trevor about that, she decided, as she only half-listened to Maude's recital.

Maude chattered on, oblivious to her sister's indifference. "Johnny just isn't old enough to swim!" she was telling Emily. "I don't hold with this nonsense of throwing them into the water as soon as they can walk. When Richard suggested it, I said 'No!', emphatically." She broke off abruptly.

"Em," she said, in a tone of faint surprise. "You look as if all this bored you to death!"

Emily shrugged and looked past Maude, wondering what had happened to Fawn. "Why, no! I'm absolutely *fascinated* by stories about your children leaping about in the water, darling," she said sarcastically.

Maude rose. "I think," she said, "I'll give mother a hand. She seems stuck with that awful Mrs. Broderick."

Benjamin, meanwhile, had had enough of the Mayor. He edged away and looked around the room.

"What is it, Daddy?" Rosamond asked quickly. "Is anything wrong?"

"No sign of Fawn?"

Rosamond bit back her disappointment. It was always Fawn or someone else that he wanted to talk to.

"When you hear the trumpets, Daddy," she said with a touch of bitterness in her voice.

And now, over all their voices, could be heard the faint ringing of a doorbell. Hacker set down his tray and moved out to the hall.

Mary still sat with Mrs. Broderick. Maude had stopped to talk to someone else after leaving Emily. From time to time Mary said, "Oh, yes," and "Really, Mrs. Broderick!" and nodded, but she was not really listening. There was a line of preoccupation across her fine forehead.

Mrs. Broderick, unaware of her hostess's inattention, wheezed on in her high voice. She was relating her impressions of the decoration of the new house of some woman in the Cecelian Guild, whose name Mary hadn't quite caught to begin with.

"It isn't as though the drapes don't match the carpets," Mrs. Broderick declared. "It's more like they clash. You know what I mean? Now, you take a color like peach—"

Mary had turned her eyes in the direction of the entranceway. They suddenly lit up. She smiled. "Ah!" she cried.

Fawn stood framed in the archway.

She was a striking figure—not that she needed anyone to tell her that. She waited for a moment until all the eyes in the room were upon her. She was very assured. The effect she made was dazzling. Her hair was bound in a vivid, flamingo-colored lace bandeau which concealed most of it. As for her gown, it was something the like of which had not yet been seen in the city of Boston. It was a glowing red and fell in long chiffon pleats, looking vaguely Greek. It left her shoulders and a good part of her breast bare.

There was a general subdued gasp, which Fawn relished for another instant. Then she advanced toward her mother as though thoroughly unaware of the stir her entrance had created.

"Oh, Mama!" she cried. "I'm sorry I'm late!" She said it as though she were reciting the opening lines of a play.

Mrs. Broderick's pale blue eyes registered every detail of what Fawn Lassiter had on. She couldn't wait for the next meeting of the Cecelian Guild. Talk about clashing colors!

When Fawn reached her mother, Mary Lassiter got to her feet and they kissed warmly.

"I love your dress, Fawn," Mary said.

"Frock, darling, frock. Dresses come from Filene's," Fawn corrected her teasingly.

"And this one? Don't tell me you sat down at the Singer machine and sewed it yourself!" Mary replied sharply.

"You'll find out soon enough," Fawn said, "when they send Daddy the bill for it!"

Her eyes roamed around the room. She caught sight of Miss Gardiner, in her serviceable dark blue dinner dress, which had all too probably come from Filene's. "How are you, Miss Gardiner?"

"Fine, thank you," Marilyn began.

But Fawn had already moved away, having flashed a smile at Mrs. Broderick's pouter-pigeon bust. She crossed the room and presented her cheek to her father to be kissed.

He said in her ear, as he kissed her, "What happened to your pet Italian? Did he ditch you?"

"Oh, Daddy!" she exclaimed, beaming a smile around the room. "He just couldn't make dinner. I'm supposed to make all kinds of Continental apologies. He'll drop by later." She caught sight of Maude, sitting on a sofa with Richard Palmer. "Maudie!" she cried. She floated toward the sofa. Her father shook his head to himself and smiled as he watched her.

Now Fawn was bending over the back to the sofa to kiss her oldest sister. Richard had leapt to his feet.

"How are you, Maude, dearest? It's been ages!" Fawn exclaimed.

"Ages," echoed Maude.

She kissed Richard. "Hello, darling Richard!" she said. "Was it nice in Florida?"

"You'll bc interested in this, Fawn!" Richard told her eagerly. "I think I've got the inside track on that Hereshoff sloop I was telling you about! It's forty-six feet—"

"Later, darling!"

Hacker had appeared at her elbow bearing his tray of drinks.

"Brandy, please," she told him. Then she turned back to Richard. "I'll be terribly interested in any sloop you want to tell me about—after I've had my brandy."

She next made her way to Emily.

The sisters greeted each other with a cool kiss. Emily was wondering if she would ever have the gall to appear in something like what Fawn was wearing.

"And where's Trevor?" Fawn asked. "I don't seem to see him."

"Stick around," Emily snapped back. "He'll find you."

Fawn gave Emily a dead stare. Then she broke into a loud, unabashed laugh.

Benjamin stood beside Rosamond. We had been following Fawn's progress with amusement, while Rosamond watched her with sullen envy. Now Benjamin pulled his watch from his pocket and consulted it. Everyone was there except for—

Mary appeared at his side. She looked worried.

"What," she asked, "is keeping Robby?"

CHAPTER TWENTY-SIX: THE EMPTY SLEEVE

Upstairs, in Robert's bedroom, O'Hara was helping him get ready.

It was a strained and silent procedure.

Robert stood in front of a mahogany-framed cheval glass, waiting for O'Hara to finish placing a black onyx cuff link in the empty sleeve of his stiff-bosomed shirt. He watched dispassionately, almost as though what O'Hara was doing had nothing whatever to do with him, personally.

Finally O'Hara managed to get the link in place in the starched cuff.

And now it was time for O'Hara to help him into his dinner jacket. The business of drawing the empty sleeve into the sleeve of the jacket was a slow one, and awkward.

Robert remained rigid and immobile, staring woodenly at his reflection in the looking glass.

"Three years old, the jacket is," O'Hara remarked, "and it still fits you like a glove, Mr. Lassiter."

"Tuck it in, will you, O'Hara?" Robert said shortly.

"Oh, yes, sir," O'Hara said.

He folded the empty sleeve into the pocket of the dinner jacket.

"How's that, Mr. Lassiter?"

Robert picked up a half-empty glass from the table and took a long gulp from it, reducing its contents to a quarter.

"Still empty," he said.

CHAPTER TWENTY-SEVEN: IN THE KITCHEN

The staff had their hands full in the kitchen that evening.

Piper, resplendent in his chef's white cap and jacket, moved like a dancer between the stove and the center table. The table was already covered with dishes which were ready to be served. Mrs. Hacker fussed over them, making sure that they were properly garnished and fit for presentation.

In addition to the regular staff, two specialists had been recruited for the dinner party. George Tibbs was the bartender the Lassiters always used when they entertained. He was a solemn young man who regularly worked as an assistant at the bar of Benjamin Lassiter's club. Now, surrounded by bottles and glasses and his tub filled with blocks of ice, he went about his duties with an air of intense concentration.

He was especially proud of having been singled out by Benjamin Lassiter. You never knew what working for a man like Lassiter might lead to!

For Emile, the Alsatian pastry cook, it was much more of a routine occasion. At the moment he was engaged in squeezing floral patterns onto a great tray of petits fours, while Brian Mallory stood at his elbow, intently observing the process.

Hacker came through the swinging door. He cast a quick professional eye over the room, exchanging a glance with Mrs. Hacker, whose nod assured him that everything was going as it should.

"Two more grape juice, Mr. Tibbs," he called out. "And another rye with soda for the Mayor."

"I'm ready any minute now, Mr. Hacker," Piper announced.

"Mr. Robert hasn't come down yet," Hacker told him.

"I don't know about Mister Robert," Piper told him, "but my lobster bisque is ready. I already put in the sherry."

Mrs. Hacker remarked as Tibbs prepared Broderick's third highball of the evening, "That's a fine mayor, breaking the law by drinking like that."

"He's not breaking the law yet, my dear," Hacker reminded her. "Not until twelve o'clock."

Brian meanwhile squinted critically at the floral creations emerging from Emile's icing gun.

"It appears to me, Emile, my man," he observed, rubbing his chin judiciously, "that the daffodil is a little lopsided."

Emile continued to squeeze yellow icing deftly onto the little glazed cakes.

"Mrs. Lowell makes no complaint about my daffodils," he replied in his heavy French accent. "Mrs. Saltonstall makes no complaints. Mrs. Jack Gardner—"

"Who're they?" Brian demanded.

Hacker's voice cut across the room.

"Brian!"

"I'm only trying hard to learn a useful trade," Brian explained.

"Try learning it with your mouth shut," Hacker told him.

"On the other hand," Brain told Emile placatingly, "the little roses are masterpieces, man. Ma-a-a-asterpieces!"

Emile beamed.

"My specialité!" he exclaimed. "The roses are very much in demand."

Hacker sped out of the room with his tray of drinks. Piper stirred the lobster bisque and frowned. Mrs. Hacker fussed with parsley and thin slices of lemon. Emile went on squeezing yellow daffodils out of his icing gun, while Brian watched in admiration.

All the same, there was an air of tension in the kitchen. They were still waiting for the signal for dinner to be served. It was already well past the usual time.

CHAPTER TWENTY-EIGHT:
A ROSE IN ROBERT'S LAPEL

Robert was nearly ready now.

"Just a moment, sir," O'Hara told him. He went to the dresser, took a wired white rose from it, and adjusted it in the lapel of Robert's dinner jacket. Then he stepped back. "Very handsome, sir," he said, eyeing Robert admiringly. "Very handsome."

Robert cast a glazed look at himself in the cheval glass. All he saw was the empty sleeve tucked into his pocket. What, he wondered, was so damned handsome about that?

He raised his glass to his lips again. It was empty. He set it down.

Robert frowned.

They were downstairs, all of them, waiting for him now. He would have to face them, sooner or later.

He went over to his dresser, pulled open the bottom drawer and found a bottle of cognac. He handed it to O'Hara. He said with a wan smile, "Another thing I cannot do is handle a corkscrew."

Reluctantly, O'Hara produced a corkscrew from his vest pocket.

Robert poured himself a substantial drink. He stood in front of the mirror, watching himself drink. For some reason the sight of the white rose in his lapel irritated him.

O'Hara stood close by, anxiously watching him.

"Shall we join the party now, sir?" he asked finally.

Robert emptied his glass and placed it with a ceremonious gesture on the table.

O'Hara waited expectantly.

They were all waiting expectantly, he told himself.

Then he made up his mind.

He strode to his closet and got a hat and his overcoat. He held the hat by placing the brim between his teeth. Then he handed the coat to O'Hara who silently held it for him as he got into it. There was another empty sleeve to tuck in.

"Yes, O'Hara," he said with a savage grin. "We'll join the party now. But not this party, O'Hara. Not this one!"

He picked up a pair of driving goggles from the dresser, then he lurched toward the door.

O'Hara stood there helplessly, watching him go.

Now, O'Hara wondered, what could he say to Mr. Hacker?

CHAPTER TWENTY-NINE: CAVIAR CANAPES

Hacker came out of the kitchen with another tray of canapes. They were caviar canapes, topped with crumbled egg yolk.

He made his way to Mary Lassiter. Rosamond had by this time taken Mrs. Broderick's place beside her.

Hacker bent over Mary with the tray.

"These are the last of the canapes, Madam," he told her in a low voice. "Piper informs me that dinner is ready."

"But we're still waiting for Mr. Robert, Hacker," she said. She glanced toward the entrance of the living room. "He should be down any minute." But there was no sign as yet of Robert.

Rosamond volunteered at once to run upstairs and see what was keeping him.

"O'Hara is with him, Miss Rosamond," Hacker said.

"Are you sure, Hacker?" She looked uneasy.

Hacker lowered his eyes.

"Are you sure, Hacker?" Rosamond repeated.

"Positive, Miss Rosamond," Hacker said, and backed away with his tray of untouched canapes. Anyway, he thought, they would finish them off in the kitchen, after everything had quieted down.

CHAPTER THIRTY: A CONVERSATION ON THE BLOWER

When Hacker returned to the kitchen with the tray of canapes, Piper was agitatedly wiping his sweating forehead with a linen napkin.

"I'm not going to reheat the soup, Mrs. Hacker," he was telling her. "That lobster bisque is too delicate. I'm not doing to *do* that!"

"Now, don't get yourself all worked up, Mr. Piper," Mrs. Hacker said. "They'll be sitting down any minute."

"And then there's those ducks," Piper fumed. "How long you think I can keep basting them? They're down to nothing but crust and bones already!"

Hacker set down his tray.

"We can't keep on serving them the canapes," he announced. "They've had enough of them already. They wouldn't touch these."

"Well?" said Mrs. Hacker.

"Call the room," he told her. "Find out what's holding him up."

As Mrs. Hacker made her way through the tables

loaded with waiting food toward the blower which hung on the far wall and which communicated with all the upstairs rooms, the apparatus suddenly emitted a wheezing sound. She ran now and picked up the receiver from its hook.

She spoke into it. "Yes?"

Then she placed it to her ear and listened for a moment.

Hacker was already at her side.

She held the apparatus out to him.

Hacker listened in turn, his face grave.

It was O'Hara, speaking from Robert's bedroom.

". . . .And I would think he's on his way to the garage," O'Hara was saying, "because he took the goggles with him."

Hacker nodded and put the blower to his mouth.

"All right, Mr. O'Hara." He had to shout. You always had to shout to make yourself heard on that thing. "Come down, Mr. O'Hara," he said. "You can lend us a hand down here."

He hung up.

He stood there, reflecting.

Mrs. Hacker signaled a question to him with her eyes, but he merely shook his head. Then, with a sigh, he straightened up and turned toward the door. It wasn't going to be easy, telling Mr. Lassiter what had happened with Mr. Robert.

His eyes suddenly opened wide.

Rosamond was standing there, just inside the swinging doors, staring at him. He could tell from the expression on her pale face that she had overheard the whole conversation.

He remained there for a moment, lingering pensively beside the blower, trying to make up his mind. All the others in the room, even Emile and Tibbs, were watching him. Then Hacker suddenly nodded his head decisively. He had thought of what had to be done.

He charged back into the room.

"Brian!" he said. "I want you!"

CHAPTER THIRTY-ONE: DINNER IS SERVED

In the living room, the Lassiters and their guests were growing restless. They had already guessed that something had gone wrong. But no one as yet had dared to say anything about it.

The groups had shifted. Benjamin and Mary Lassiter now stood with the Brodericks. The Mayor was laughing heartily at a slightly off-color joke of his own. Mrs. Broderick has pasted a smile on her thin lips. She was hoping that they wouldn't serve any more drinks. Broderick had already had more than enough. Mary looked anxiously across the Brodericks at Benjamin. Benjamin withdrew his gold watch from his vest pocket for the twentieth time and consulted it.

Hacker appeared and discreetly raised his eyebrows at Benjamin, who left the group.

The Mayor had already embarked on one of his stories about Calvin Coolidge, one which they had all heard before.

"I never did have much faith in the Governor," he was saying in his loud bluff voice, "and when he made that crack—"

Mary was not listening to him. Her eyes were following Benjamin and Hacker. She saw them retreat to a corner of the room. Hacker was murmuring something into Benjamin's ear.

"I knew I was right about him all the time," Broderick declared, unaware of the fact that no one was listening to him. "No sense of humor, just no sense of—"

He was interrupted by Benjamin's voice calling across the room, "All right, everybody. Dinner. Dinner is served!"

There was a general stir, and a surge toward the dining room doors, which Hacker had opened.

Mary Lassiter moved as quickly as she could, with the help of her ebony cane, toward Benjamin's side.

He took her arm and led her toward the dining room.

"I don't understand," she whispered. "Why are we starting without Robby? What was Hacker saying to you?"

"He was informing me that Mr. Robert will be down shortly." He squeezed her arm. "Now, Mary, will you stop worrying?"

They looked up, smiling, and led their guests into the dining room.

CHAPTER THIRTY-TWO: BEARCAT

The former stable and carriage house behind the Louisburg Square mansion had, some years previously, been converted into a garage. Fawn had stormed about that, saying that she needed it for a studio. This was in the days when she was being passionate about becoming a painter, but practical considerations had prevailed over Fawn's artistic career. A studio for Fawn had been rented on Tea Wharf, only to be abandoned a year later when Fawn had tired of dabbling in paints. Curiously enough, the ebbing of her interest had coincided with her teacher's moving to New York.

The garage had remained.

It now housed three cars: the Packard limousine, a long touring car (also a Packard) and a little red Stutz. The Stutz was the famous Bearcat model with the bucket seats. It wasn't really a practical car, or even a comfortable one, but it had been widely publicized as being the last word in motorcars, and so the Lassiters had bought one for Robert. It had been waiting for him when he came home from France.

And now, in his dinner jacket, and with the white rose

in his buttonhole, his hat set on the back of his head, Robert was vainly trying to start it by cranking it.

Damn that empty sleeve!

Rosamond suddenly appeared in the open doorway. A coat was thrown over her shoulders. She had grabbed the first one she had seen, which had happened to be Mrs. Broderick's monkey fur-trimmed cloak. All the same, she was shivering.

"Robert!" Rosamond cried. "What do you think you're doing?" She stared at him, ashen-faced. "Everyone is waiting for you!"

He paid no attention to her. At that moment the engine suddenly sputtered and started up. He quickly moved to the door, flung the crank to the floor and started to get into the car.

Rosamond ran forward and clutched his arm.

"Rob!" she pleased. "Please!"

He roughly pulled his arm free, forcing his sister against the wall.

And then someone else had stepped up from behind and grabbed him by the shoulder.

"Oh, no you don't!" a voice said.

Robert turned. "Who the hell—?" he began. Then he saw Brian Mallory's thin set face thrust into his. "Oh," he said. "It's you. What do you mean, 'Oh, no'?"

"I mean," said Brian firmly, "oh, no, you can't be thinking of driving this automobile."

"Are you telling me—" Robert's face flushed with anger. "Are you trying to—?"

"Yes," Brian said. "I'm telling you. And for two very good reasons. First, you're drunk, man. Second, you've only got one arm."

Rosamond gasped.

"How dare you?" she cried in outrage.

Brian did not even turn to look at her. "How do you expect to drive and shift with one drunken arm?" he said quietly to Robert. Robert gave him a fuddled stare. "Have you ever tried it?" Brian went on.

Robert continued to stare at him.

"Well," said Brian, "I won't have you try it now. For you sake and mine. I don't want you to kill yourself and I don't want to lose me job!"

"What job?" demanded Rosamond. "You don't work here!"

"No," he admitted. "But I'm talkin' about the job I might get as a reward if I stop the young master of the house from going out into the night in this thing and destroying himself with it." He took a breath. "You read about things like that in books," he said.

Robert dug into his coat pocket and pulled out his wallet. It was stuffed with bills.

"I tell you what," he said. "I'll give you some money. How much do you want? And you can just go out and have a good time all by—"

"Put it away, Mr. Lassiter. I am a man who can resist all temptation." He flashed a quick smile at Rosamond. "Your sister here will testify to that."

Robert glared at Brian. Then, awkwardly, he shoved the wallet back into his pocket.

"That's more like it, Mr. Lassiter," Brian said.

Suddenly Robert made a lunge for the door of the car. It was surprisingly quick.

Brian, however, grabbed him in time and held him back.

"Let go of me!" Robert protested. "Take your hands off me!" He struggled in Brian's grip. He was strong, but Brian's grip was even stronger.

"Wait!" Brian said. "Just wait, wait, wait!" He grinned persuasively. "Can we discuss a compromise, in the manner of reasonable men?"

Robert stopped struggling after a moment.

"What compromise?" he wanted to know.

"I'll drive you," Brian proposed. "Just say where you want to go."

Rosamond said fiercely, "You're not driving him anywhere!"

Brian loosened his grip and Robert freed himself. He straightened his bow tie, regarding Brian with a look of new interest.

"You know how to drive?" he asked.

"Robert!" Rosamond called out in warning.

"Drive?" said Brian. He pushed out his lower lip cockily. "I was, for three years running, the champion—"

Robert cut him short.

"Get in," he ordered.

Brian climbed in behind the wheel while Rosamond looked helplessly on. Robert squeezed in beside him.

"Nothing to fear, Rosie," Brian called out to her. "He's with me." He turned to Robert. "Now, would you tell me, just to get it straight, is that the first shift?"

"That's first," Robert told him, nodding.

"Then we're off," Brian shouted. The Bearcat zoomed out of the garage, over the cobbles and out into the street.

Rosamond stared after it, clutching Mrs. Brodcrick's cloak around her shoulders. Then, with the cold January wind whipping at her long skirts, she managed to get the garage doors to close. If only, she thought, she had an inkling as to where the two of them were going in the Bearcat! But there was no knowing, ever, with her brother Robert, any more.

Shivering, she made her way back to the house and the dinner party.

CHAPTER THIRTY-THREE: PINK SHADES AND YELLOW CHRYSANTHEMUMS

The Lassiter dining room was a blaze of light. Light came from the crystal chandelier which hung over the center of the big table and from the silver candelabra: two of them on the main table and another on the second, smaller table, which had been set up in a corner of the room. Each of the candelabra was adorned with little pink fringed shades which turned the light into a warm flattering glow.

It was a massive room. The floral wallpaper was vaguely Jacobean with a suggestion of William Morris. It had been there when the Lassiters had bought the house. The chairs were in the Chippendale style, as was the dining table, now covered with a floor-length lace-trimmed cloth.

Mr. Faber's yellow chrysanthemums were everywhere, arranged in tasteful garlands down the table's center and in a great glowing sunburst from a silver urn on the mahogany sideboard.

The table was set with gold-rimmed Limoges porcelain and heavy silver in an ornate design. At each setting there was an array of glittering Waterford goblets. The damask napkins had been folded to suggest birds in flight, and in the center of each had been tucked a place card with the appropriate name written out in Marilyn Gardiner's beautifully round Palmer Method script.

Hacker and the maids served the oysters. After that came the lobster bisque which, in spite of Piper's despairing concern, had not required reheating. Then, when the soup plates had been cleared away, celery and stuffed olives and salted almonds appeared. The room rang with talk.

And then it was time to serve the ducks: canvasbacks, prepared *a la* Delmonico, on a bed of wild rice.

In spite of Robert's absence, which had been noted but not mentioned, and Rosamond's, which no one seemed to be aware of, things seemed to be going well. Mary and Benjamin Lassiter exchanged a look across the table's length. Mary nodded.

Benjamin got to his feet and tapped his wine goblet sharply with the dull edge of a knife.

The conversation died down. Even Fawn stopped talking. All eyes were turned to Benjamin.

"I'm not going to make a speech," he announced. He added, beaming genially, "Not a long one, anyway. So just go right on eating, all of you, please. Please! I'm standing up now just to say 'Welcome!' to our guests and to my children and to my children-in-law. I want to tell you how happy your mother and I are to be back in the Land of the Free and in the great city of Boston and in the bosom of the family." There was an appreciative murmur. Smiling, Benjamin held up a hand until the murmur subsided. "Since we have picked a historic night for this gathering," he went on, "I would like to offer an appropriate sentiment for the first toast of the evening." He raised his glass. "Ladies, gentlemen," he cried. "To the passing of the old-fashioned saloon!"

The men around the table rose to their feet. "Amen!"

and "Hear, hear!" they shouted. Someone gave out a loud and expressive groan which was greeted with a burst of laughter. Everyone drank.

It was just as they were drinking to the passing of the old-fashioned saloon that Rosamond unobtrusively glided into the room and quietly took her place at the smaller table.

CHAPTER THIRTY-FOUR: AN OLD-FASHIONED SALOON

At the very moment when Benjamin Lassiter and his guests on Beacon Hill were drinking to the passing of the old-fashioned saloon, in another, less opulent section of the city of Boston, and in one of the old-fashioned saloons whose very death knell was being rung that night throughout the United States, a somewhat less sedate scene was taking place.

It was a typical specimen, this particular saloon, of a drinking parlor in a working-class neighborhood of Boston. There was sawdust on the floor. It had an immense bar with a lavish free-lunch counter, dark paneling, elaborately engraved mirrors and three burly bartenders.

At the moment the saloon was crowded. It was filled with smoke and the fumes of beer and whisky. It was also very noisy. Everyone was there to have a good time. It was like a wake: an occasion for a boisterous, never-to-be-forgotten farewell. And the bartenders were being worked to death.

There was a sudden uproar in the middle of the bar. Hands reached out to lift a portly man in a battered derby hat from the floor to the bar. Everyone started shouting at once. "It's Paddy!" "Hooray for old Paddy!" they called encouragingly. It was obvious that Paddy was expected to deliver a word or two.

Paddy raised his plump white hands for silence.

"Now, then," he began in the thick brogue of a professional Irishman, "I have some good news for you all. Believe it or not, there is some good news on this black night. On behalf of the management, I want to tell you that at the rate we're going, we'll never empty every bottle in the house by midnight." This statement was greeted by protests and loud cries of dismay. Paddy held up his hands again. "So," he announced, "I'm offering an incentive to every serious drinker in the house. From now on—all drinks are on the house!"

There was a thunderous roar of approval. Glasses were held high. The bartenders began pouring and spilling and splashing liquor into them.

Paddy shouted over the din.

"I think—a little quietness, please! Thank you, gentlemen!—I think it is only fitting and proper that we start off this part of the evening with a toast to some of the great men who have leaned their bellies up against this very bar in the past!"

There was a sudden hush.

"First of all," Paddy said with solemnity, tipping his refilled glass and nodding to a portrait of a staring man with drooping moustaches which hung on the wall behind him, "I ask you to join me in a tribute to the dear, departed and well-beloved James F.X. Slattery, councilman from this district for forty glorious years!"

Everyone drank to James F.X. Slattery.

The glasses were promptly replenished.

"Next," Paddy's voice rang out across the bar, "a toast to Francis Patrick Dugan, the finest Congressman ever to represent the 19th in the sacred halls of Congress in Washington, D.C." He raised his eyes reverently to the stamped tin ceiling. "I thank God," he said, "that he never lived to see this night." He tipped his glass to a beefy, red-faced man who was standing in the front line. "Your father, Tim," he said, "and my friend!"

The toast was drunk in respectful silence.

Timothy Dugan stood there, his shoulders heaving, his eyes filling with tears. Suddenly he turned, ashamed to be seen this way, a middle-aged man convulsed with drunken sorrow at the recollection of his father, now five years gone. He fought his way through the swinging doors, not waiting to hear in whose honor Paddy's next toast was being proposed.

The doors of the saloon swung open before him, and Timothy Dugan burst out into the bitter January night. He began sobbing, great hefty sobs for the old man (Oh, there'd never be his like again!) and then at the terrible realization that tomorrow night the neighborhood saloon would be locked, barred, and closed down tight according to the letter of the law. And where could a man go then on a Saturday night to swallow a bit of cheer and get away from the wife and kids at home?

As he stood there on the sidewalk, feeling sorry for himself, twice an orphan (first the old man, and now the saloon) he heard the approaching sound of drumbeats. Pulling out an enormous red engineer's handkerchief, he wiped his eyes and blew his nose. Then he looked up to see what was happening.

Holy Mother of God! It was a funeral, and at this time of the night! Couldn't they wait until daylight and bury the corpse decently? Ah, he told himself, it was all these foreigners and pagan blacks moving into the neighborhood, changing everything from the way it was, turning night into day. There was no knowing where it would end!

All the same, he ceremoniously removed his hat and watched the cortege. A black-draped horse, led by a man in a black silk stovepipe hat and black armband, pulled the wagon. There were black plumes on the horse's head. An enormous coffin, also draped in black, sat in the middle of the wagon. Mourners marched along on both sides of the bier, all with silk hats and black armbands. A drummer, beating out a lugubrious tattoo on a drum draped in black, brought up the rear.

"God rest his soul, whoever he is!" Timothy Dugan murmured solemnly.

As he crossed himself, he caught sight of the banner nailed across the coffin. "JOHN BARLEYCORN. R.I.P.," it said. And then there was a crowd of kids, dressed up in old hats and outsize dresses and old frock coats, following the wagon, dancing the cakewalk and singing and shouting. Some of them carried torches which lit up the street with their lurid light.

He watched until the procession reached the corner, where it created a small traffic snarl. He saw a little red sports car, one of those Stutzes, with two men inside it, come to a halt in the middle of the street, its horn blowing impatiently, waiting for the funeral cortege to pass. And then, when the black-plumed horses and its wagon with the coffin on it, and the mourners and the dancing kids had passed, the Bearcat spurted forward and shot out of sight.

CHAPTER THIRTY-FIVE: ROBERT JOINS THE REVELRY

Following Robert's direction, Brian Mallory drove the Bearcat through the dark streets of Boston. After being held up for a few minutes by John Barleycorn's funeral procession, he rounded a far corner and proceeded slowly down a street of shabby brownstone houses.

"Stop here!" Robert called out.

He indicated a house which seemed less shabby than its neighbors. Its shades were all drawn. Through the window, however, they could hear the music from inside.

Brian pulled up beside the curb.

Robert jumped out onto the sidewalk.

He turned to Brian, whose legs were already halfway out of the car.

"And just where do you think you're going?" he demanded.

"With you," said Brian.

"Not a chance," Robert said. "This is a private party I'm going to. You wait in the car."

"It's a hell of a cold night," Brian reminded him.

"Then go home!"

He went bounding up the steps.

Brian got out of the car and stood beside it, peering after him.

He saw Robert make it to the top step and then lean on the doorbell. After a long wait, the curtain over the window in the door was pulled aside. There was the face of a little black maid squinting through the glass. When she saw Robert she pulled the curtain back across the window.

"Hey!" Robert yelled. "Open the door, will you? Where are you going? Open the damned door for me!" He started pounding on it with his one hand.

After a while Brian saw the door being opened and a stately black woman in a Nile green evening gown filled the doorway.

"Hullo, Hortense!" Robert greeted her.

She cast an anxious glance up and down the street.

"What's the matter with you?" she said sternly. "Makin' all that noise and fuss?"

"Tarbaby won't let me in," Robert said.

Hortense pointed to Brian, who had left the car by now and was standing at the bottom of the flight of steps, watching them.

"Who's that?"

"He's only my chauffeur," Robert told her. He started to push his way past her, but she held her position, a hand on each of the door jambs.

"What's this?" he demanded. "The Battle of the Marne? 'They shall not pass,' eh?"

"That's right, Mister," Hortense said grimly. "They shall not pass."

He raised his voice. "Let me in Hortense," he warned, "or you'll hear some real *noise!*"

Reluctantly, she stepped aside.

From where he stood, Brian could hear the band playing inside, and the sound of revelry. When the door closed behind Robert and Hortense, it grew much fainter, but he could still hear it. Someone was singing in a loud throaty contralto.

Robert stood in the vestibule, a step or two behind Hortense. The little black maid hovered wide-eyed in the background. Through the closed door which led to the parlor Robert could hear the sounds of the party which was going on behind it. It seemed to be coming from very far away, but it sounded like a good party and nothing was going to stop him from joining it.

Hortense swung around and confronted him.

"Mr. Brown," she said, "didn't your friend tell you? I don't want you comin' here."

"Why not?" he asked belligerently. "What's the matter with me?"

"Nothing's the matter with you," she said. "It's only your *name* that's the matter."

He stared at her through the fuddled haze.

"You know my name, huh?"

Hortense majestically adjusted one of the tortoise-shell combs in her towering hairdo.

"Damned right I know it!" she said.

"Well, why should that make any difference? I'm not going to make any trouble for you."

"I know you ain't," Hortense conceded. "I know you're a gentleman. But I don't want nobody else finding out you come to my place."

"Like who?" he asked, frowning.

"Nobody else like your daddy, for instance," Hortense replied.

"Hortense," he pleaded. He managed to smile at her ingratiatingly. "I *like* it here—"

"I like to hear that, Mister," she said. "But," she added firmly, "I'm sorry."

There was a long pause. He stared at her in silence. Then he suddenly exploded. "The hell you are!" he shouted, and lunged past her, pushing open the door to the parlor.

The room was crowded. Hortense had hired a three-piece band for the evening, to supplement the piano player. The dance floor was filled with couples, the space in front of the bar was packed two-deep. Now the music suddenly broke off. The dancers stood staring at him. The drinkers remained at the bar, their glasses suspended in midair, their faces turned in his direction.

Across the well of sudden silence a voice called out, "What's going on?"

At the rear of the parlor rose a long staircase. Now, standing on the landing, Harry Emmet appeared in his striped shirt, without a collar and tie, his vest unbuttoned.

"What's going on?" he called again. "Do you need me for anything, Hortense?"

"Harry!" Robert cried.

Emmet raced down the stairs.

"What are you doing here? I told you—"

"Mr. Smith," Hortense stormed, "I tried to explain to your friend that—"

"I'll take care of it, Hortense," Emmet said.

"Where the devil have you been?" Robert said. "I've been trying to get hold of you all day!"

"Friday's my day off," Emmet replied impatiently. "You know that."

"I *knew*. But I've been trying to get hold of you."

"Well, now you found me, what's the emergency?" Emmet asked.

Robert suddenly looked boyish and uncertain.

"You're not mad?"

Emmet shook his head. "No," he said. "I'm not mad."

"I'm glad about that, Harry," Robert said.

Emmet took him by the arm. "What's the trouble?" he asked.

"Well, I didn't want to go to that dinner party," Robert began.

"Oh," groaned Emmet. "Jeeezus!"

"I'd rather go out on the town with you, Harry. Especially tonight!"

Emmet turned to Hortense.

She shook her head emphatically.

"Uh-uh," she said.

"Come on, Hortense!" he cajoled. "Don't be like that. It's a second New Year's Eve! Here's a man wants to join the party. Are you going to throw him out in the cold? Hell, it ain't a fit night out for man or beast!"

The others in the room, realizing that nothing serious or interesting was going to happen after all, had gone back to their dancing and drinking. The music resumed with a loud, catchy ragtime beat. A middle-aged man wearing a paper hat, with streamers draped around his shoulders like a multicolored boa, danced in front of them, dragging a dark girl in a red dress after him.

"Happy Prohibition!" he shouted in Robert's ear.

The girl pulled him away, up the stairs and out of sight.

"Come on, Hortense," Emmet begged. "What d'you say? Just this one last time!"

Hortense stood there, wavering.

"Hortense?" Robert said, eyeing her anxiously.

"Oh," she said at last. "What the hell!"

"Atta girl!" Robert cried. He tossed his hat in the air and went to join the revelry.

"But remember," Hortense called after him. "This is positively the last time, Mr. Brown!"

CHAPTER THIRTY-SIX: BRIAN MAKES A TELEPHONE CALL

A slender figure walked down the street, hands shoved deep into the pockets of his corduroy trousers, his shoulders hunched against the cold wind. A knitted scarf was wound around his neck. He was not wearing an overcoat, although he could have well used one, if he had owned it.

It was Brian Mallory.

He had left the Bearcat parked in front of Hortense's house. He knew that he had to do something about Robert Lassiter. The question was: how to go about it?

From a basement stairway a man and woman in flashy clothes surged out onto the street. Each carried a bottle. They were singing loudly, but the words were indistinct. They weaved their way toward him.

"Come on and have a drink with us!" the man bawled. "Tonight's the last chance, my friend, to have a friendly little drink without breaking the law!"

Brian stepped off the sidewalk to get out of their way.

He turned the corner and went on.

He had gone on for several blocks without finding what he was looking for. All the stores were closed, their fronts boarded up in anticipation of possible window smashing.

And then he saw bright lights and gold lettering on the plate glass windows which announced that it was Patrick J. Shea's Saloon and Bar.

It was like a ship in the middle of an empty ocean of darkness.

He studied the façade for a moment or two. Then he went inside, through the swinging doors.

The tumult and the shouting had died down. Some of the customers sat dejectedly at the tables. A number of them had slid down to the accommodating sawdust on the floor. A few were draped over the bar, where Paddy Shea sat, his derby hat well back on his head, clutching a nearly empty bottle. The old customer nearest him was weeping silently.

Paddy was still reminiscing.

"And, oh yes!" he recalled. "There was the time when Teddy Roosevelt, no less, stopped in here to sample the pig's knuckles. Teddy Roosevelt himself!" Paddy raised his bottle. "To Teddy Roosevelt!"

He took a hearty swig. A few of the faithful were still in a state to be able to drink along with him.

Brian stepped over several prone customers and reached the bar.

"You got one of them telephones?" he asked.

Paddy stared at him.

He cupped his ear and leaned closer to Brian.

"Do I hear the spoken music of County Limerick?" he inquired.

"You do," Brian assured him. "All the way from Ballybunion to Tipperary."

Paddy waved his arm expansively.

"The house will stand the cost of the telephone call," he declared. He plinked the cash register and removed a nickel from the cash tray which he handed over ceremoniously to Brian. "Five cents on the house!" Paddy announced.

"Thank you," Brian said. "And where is it?"

Paddy pointed vaguely to a spot behind the bar. Then he raised his voice and his bottle. "And then let us not forget our old friend John Bradford Bigelow. He may have been a dirty Protestant, but—"

Brian left him to finish his toast and made his way to the telephone.

CHAPTER THIRTY-SEVEN: BENJAMIN LASSITER GOES DOWN TO THE CORNER FOR A BEER

The Lassiters' dinner was going smoothly.

In the kitchen, Mrs. Hacker, Piper, Tibbs and Emile supervised their separate corners. O'Hara moved among them, lending assistance wherever it was required. Eleanor and Kate and Maureen moved efficiently between the dining room and the kitchen, carrying out platters of food and returning with empty dishes.

Hacker appeared.

"We can pass the duck around once more," he announced. "They need more of the guava jelly. And what about the alligator pear salad? Is it ready?"

"Ready and waiting," Piper said.

"Right, Mr. Hacker," Eleanor said.

"The girls are doing very well indeed," he informed her.

"Thank you, Mr. Hacker," she said, looking pleased.

Mrs. Hacker looked up from the silver dish on which she was arranging wafers for the cheese course.

"Has she asked about Mr. Robert again?"

Hacker shook his head.

"But *he* keeps looking at his watch," he said.

"I don't know—" began Mrs. Hacker, only to be interrupted by the loud ringing of the telephone.

O'Hara raced to grab the receiver.

"Lassiter residence," he announced. His voice was a startlingly accurate imitation of Hacker's. Then, "Yes, Brian!" he said, in his own voice. He held the receiver out to Hacker.

Hacker took it at once.

"Yes, Brian?" he asked. He listened for a moment, then he nodded. He looked around, still listening. All work in the kitchen had been suspended. They were all staring at him. He gestured to them to get on with their work. They did so, but their attention remained riveted on the telephone conversation.

"Hold on, Brian," Hacker said. "Don't go away, whatever you do." He left the receiver dangling. For a long instant he regarded the wall, as if seeing nothing. Then he nodded his head abruptly and strode out of the kitchen.

He made his way directly to the head of the table. He bent over Benjamin and whispered something in his ear.

Mary, at the opposite end of the table, had Mayor Broderick seated at her right. She was smiling automatically at him, but her gaze was fixed in Benjamin's direction.

Broderick picked up his wine glass. He sipped and smacked his lips. "I'll say one thing, Mrs. Lassiter. Your husband still has the best cellar in Boston!"

She smiled at him, unhearing. She saw Benjamin nod to Hacker. Then he turned and murmured something to Mrs. Broderick, after which he pushed back his chair and rose from the table. Hacker followed him out of the dining room.

Mary watched it all, frowning.

"He'll keep it, of course?" Broderick was saying.

She turned back to him.

"Keep what?" she asked, startled.

Broderick wiped his moustache with his napkin.

"The wine cellar!" he said.

"Oh, yes," she answered vaguely.

From where she sat she could see Benjamin and Hacker going toward the doorway which led to the living room. What, she wondered anxiously, was going on? Was Robby all right? "Dear God," she whispered under her breath. "Don't let anything happen to Robby!"

Broderick was still talking away on her right.

"He can claim," he was saying, "that he uses it for medicinal purposes!" He let out a hearty chuckle. "Of course," he added, "he's got enough medicine down there for a hospital."

Benjamin, meanwhile, had gone to his study, where he picked up the telephone. Hacker remained standing at his side.

"Brian?"

"Yes, Mr. Lassiter," said Brian's voice. He began talking at once.

"Yes," Lassiter said. "Yes." Then, "I see."

". . . As drunk as a monk," Brian went on. "In the second place, Mr. Lassiter, he's carrying the devil knows how much money with him, and frankly, Mr. Lassiter, sir, this doesn't look like the kind of place where you walk in not only drunk, but loaded down with dollars, and expect to come out on anything but a stretcher."

"Why?" Benjamin broke in. "What's it look like? What kind of a place is it?"

"Well, I'm no expert in the American style in these matters, Mr. Lassiter, but it looks like a cathouse to me."

"Why the hell did you let him go in there alone?" Benjamin shouted into the mouthpiece.

"Who the hell gave me any instructions to do otherwise?" Brian shouted back. "And why the hell are you bawling me out when I'm only doing my best to be helpful?"

"All right, Brian. Give me the address. That neighborhood? What's he doing there? Never mind. I'll meet you there in fifteen minutes. Out front. Wait for me, and don't do anything until I get there."

He hung up and started for the door.

Before he reached it, however, it had opened. Mary stalked into the room as Hacker passed into the hall.

"Something's happened to Robby!" she cried.

"No," he said.

"Don't lie to me!"

"Nothing's happened to Robby. He's all right. I'm going out now to bring him home."

"What do you mean, bring him home? Why isn't he capable of coming home himself? What's happened to him?"

Benjamin strode out into the hall. Hacker was standing there, holding Benjamin's coat and hat.

Mary had followed him. "I'm coming with you!" she said.

Benjamin savagely thrust his arms into the sleeves of his coat, assisted by Hacker.

"You are not coming with me," he told her in a firm voice. "You have guests. If they ask you where I am, tell them that I've gone down to the corner for a beer."

Hacker opened the front door, and Benjamin dashed through it out into the street.

Mary stood there, leaning heavily on her cane, staring after him.

Then she slowly turned to Hacker.

"What's happened to Robby?"

"Mr. Robert, Madam?" Hacker asked. His face was expressionless and bland. "Has something happened to Mr. Robert?"

Mary clenched her hand around the silver head of her cane.

"It's a house full of marvelous liars!" she cried. She bit her lips. "Oh, my God!" she muttered in despair, under her breath.

Hacker came forward then.

He said, quietly, "Let me offer you my arm, Madam. I am sure that you will want to go back to your guests now."

She closed her eyes for a moment. Then she reached for Hacker's proferred arm.

CHAPTER THIRTY-EIGHT: MAUDE THANKS GOD

The dinner proceeded. The alligator pear salad was served. Then the tables were cleared for dessert, which consisted of individual portions of charlotte glacé with preserved ginger. After that came the cheese, Brie and Camembert.

Mary sat silently through it all, her thoughts out in the night with Robert. Where had Benjamin gone? And why did he have to bring Robert home?

All around her there was a hubbub of conversation and occasional laughter. At her left her son-in-law, Richard Palmer, was talking to Marilyn Gardiner. Mr. Broderick, fortunately, was engaged for the moment with Emily, on his right.

"... And it draws a good four feet," Richard was saying animatedly to Marilyn Gardiner, "which is quite a bit, of course, but not in those waters, not in *those* waters."

Marilyn listened politely, sitting stiffly self-conscious beside him and picking out salted almonds from the silver dish in front of her. Her head and neck were rigid, but her eyes were busy, looking right and left along the table.

They came to rest at last on Fawn and Trevor Bullock who were seated side by side.

Fawn had just said something in an undertone which made Trevor throw his head back and burst into laughter. Marilyn wished she could have heard what Fawn had said, but the only thing she could make out was Richard's voice, enthusiastically droning on.

"All she really needs is a new spinnaker," he was saying.

Marilyn's attention wandered back to Fawn and Trevor. Trevor had just said something which made Fawn giggle, prettily and uncontrollably.

"You can't get better canvas than Bollingen makes," Richard pursued earnestly. "I mean, you can search the world over, but you will not find a better quality of canvas."

Marilyn's gaze shifted to Emily.

Emily had been watching Fawn and Trevor. If looks could kill, Marilyn reflected, Emily's rapier glance would have transfixed the two of them on the spot.

It was time to turn back to Richard. She could not think of anything to say about sails, so she merely smiled at Richard.

Encouraged by her smile, he plunged on. "Did I ever tell you about the yawl I bought immediately after the war? It was a thirty-six footer, and I got it from Barry Belcher's yard."

While he went on to describe the yawl in every detail, Marilyn's eyes wandered again. They came to a sudden stop. Maude Palmer was smiling at her, directly across the table.

"He is a bore, isn't he?" Maude remarked.

Marilyn stared at her, nonplussed.

"What did you say, Mrs. Palmer?"

"He's a dreadful bore," Maude said. She turned and glanced significantly for a moment in the direction of

Fawn and Trevor. Then she regarded her husband through the floral arrangement and the branches of the silver epergne. She gave him an indulgent smile. "For which I say," she added devoutly, "thank God!"

And then Mary Lassiter rose.

It was the signal for them all to leave the table and move into the living room, where coffee would be served.

CHAPTER THIRTY-NINE: AN OLD IRISH RECIPE

The red Stutz Bearcat was still parked at the curb in front of Hortense's house when the taxicab, with Benjamin Lassiter in it, came down the street.

Benjamin got out. As he was paying the driver, Brian emerged from the Bearcat.

Together they proceeded toward the house. Neither of them said a word to the other.

Suddenly a disheveled man materialized from behind a lamppost. He waved the two bottles which he held at them, and came toward them unsteadily. "Hey, you guys!" he shouted hoarsely. "Get down to Reilly's! They're giving it away at Reilly's. Giving it away!"

He staggered off down the street, spreading the news.

Benjamin and Brian started up the steps. Brian was the first to reach the front door. He pressed his thumb against the bell, keeping it there until the window curtain was drawn slightly back.

The little maid's black face peered out at them. She squinted at Brian and shook her head. He kept on ringing. She waved her hand at him, motioning to him to go away. Then she vanished.

Brian rang the bell again. When nothing happened, he started pounding on the door with his fists.

"Open up," he shouted. "Damn it, open up!" He turned to Benjamin. "That's the way your boy got in, by banging on the door." He resumed his hammering. "Open up!" he yelled. "It's too damned cold out here!"

Once again the curtain was drawn back. This time it was Hortense's face which appeared behind the glass.

"Hello there!" Brian said. "Remember me?"

Hortense shook her head.

"Open up, or I'll give you cause to!" he told her.

She opened the door then.

"What do you want?" she said sharply.

"Nothing much," said Brian. "We just want—"

Benjamin stepped forward, brushing Brian aside.

"My name," he said, "is Benjamin Lassiter."

Hortense's jaw fell. She stepped back. "Oh, good Lord in heaven!" she gasped.

The two men walked past her and went inside.

"I knew it would happen!" she murmured. "I just knew it!"

The band was playing "Under the Bamboo Tree," and Hortense's guests joined in with the girls, gleefully shouting the refrain:

"If you lak-a me,
Like I lak-a you . . ."

Hortense was at Benjamin's elbow.

"Mr. Lassiter, I don't want to . . ."

"Where is he?" he demanded curtly.

"Upstairs. I'll go . . ."

"Which room?" he asked in the same brusque tone.

"Don't you want me to . . ."

He was already making for the stairs. He turned. "Which room?"

"Second on the right," Hortense told him. She was already resigned and steeling herself for the consequences.

Benjamin marched steadily up the stairs, Brian keeping close behind him. There was a light on at the landing. When they reached the second door on the right, Benjamin paused and drew a long breath. Then he knocked.

"What is it?" called a man's voice from inside the room.

Without answering, Benjamin turned the knob and went in.

Brian followed at his heels.

The room was stuffy, with dark paper and a large mirror in a gilt frame on the walls. There was a glass-shaded lamp beside the rumpled bed. Harry Emmet, a bathrobe thrown over his shoulders, sat in a purple plush armchair. At his feet, in a flimsy pink shift, sat Viola. Emmet was pulling bills out of his wallet and counting them into the girl's extended hand.

Emmet glanced up to see Benjamin and Brian coming toward him. Hortense had climbed the stairs behind them and stood puffing in the doorway.

"Mr. Lassiter!"

Emmet hurriedly got to his feet, drawing the bathrobe around him and stuffing the wallet into his pocket. He yanked the girl to her feet.

"What're you doing here, Mr. Lassiter?" He gave Viola a push. "Get out of here!" he told her. "Go on. Beat it!"

He pulled her to the door, past Hortense, and shoved her out into the corridor.

Then he turned and faced Benjamin.

"I never expected to see *you* off limits, Mr. Lassiter!" he blustered.

Benjamin eyed him grimly.

"Where's my son?"

"Robert?" Emmet gave a nervous laugh. "Are you kidding, Mr. Lassiter? What would Robert be doing in a place like this?"

The singing welled up from the parlor:

"Oh, the moonlight shines tonight along the Wabash,
From the fields there comes the scent of new-mown hay . . ."

Brian's voice called out. "Mr. Lassiter!"

He had opened a door which led to a room adjoining the one they were standing in.

Benjamin cast a furious look at Emmet and went to join Brian. They stood there in the doorway, staring at the brass bed on which Robert lay sprawled.

"He's out like a light," Brian said after a moment. "We'd better let him sleep it off where he is."

"His mother is waiting for me to bring him home," Benjamin said. "And I'm going to."

"His mother," Brian repeated thoughtfully. "Well, then we'll have to see to it that he gets home, won't we?"

He whirled around.

"Where's your bathtub?" he shot at Hortense.

She looked blankly at him.

"Bathtub, woman! Where you take a bath. Back home in Ireland, I was told that America was full of them!"

She pointed to a door beyond the bed. "It's through there," she said in a low voice.

Brian lost no time in opening the door. There came, almost instantaneously, the sound of water gushing from a tap.

Brian reappeared.

"Have you also got a kitchen?"

"A kitchen? I got a great big one," she said. "Yes, indeed."

"All right then," he ordered. "I want some tabasco sauce, two eggs and some ice. Can you remember that?"

"I'll get it for you right away," she said.

"Wait a minute," he told her. "Would you have any oysters?"

"All you like. Bluepoints," she said.

"I'd like two."

"Two," she repeated. "You can have more."

"Just two," he said. "All right then."

Hortense turned to go.

"Oh," Brian called out. "There's one more ingredient!"

"You name it, Mister," she said.

"A little tincture of iodine," Brian told her.

She stared at him open-mouthed. "That's one mixture I never heard of!"

"It's an old Irish recipe I learned from my mother," Brian shot back. "Go on, now. You get all those things for me, promptly, and maybe Mr. Lassiter will see to it that you're not sent up for life imprisonment."

Hortense left them there, closing the door behind her.

Brian unwound his scarf and threw it down on the bed. After that he removed his jacket and unbuttoned his vest. They landed on the bed a moment later. Then, with a grimly businesslike expression on his lean face, he rolled up his shirt sleeves.

CHAPTER FORTY: THE FIRST STEP

Downstairs, the band was still playing and the singing was still going on. They could hear it through the closed door.

Brian finished rolling up his sleeves. He turned to Benjamin.

"Now, Mr. Lassiter," he said, "I'd like to be left alone with the drunk."

Benjamin's faced flushed. "Don't call him a drunk!" he said angrily.

"That's what he is!" retorted Brian. "You have to call a spade a spade, and to his face! That's the first step on the road to sobriety."

The flush on Benjamin's face slowly subsided.

"All right," he said calmly. "And the second step? What's that?"

"Undress the drunk," Brian said. "Then you drop him into a cold tub."

"Cold!" Benjamin exclaimed, frowning.

"As cold as you can get it," affirmed Brian, shutting the door of the second bedroom in his face.

Benjamin stood there, trying to make up his mind whether or not to fling the door open and see what was going on. He decided, finally, to let Brian take care of the job.

"Mr. Lassiter!"

Emmet had managed to pull on most of his clothes. He was surreptitiously buttoning up the fly-front of his trousers. The bathrobe had fallen to the floor. He kicked it under the bed.

Benjamin turned. He had forgotten, for the moment, about Emmet.

He paused. Then he said, "Let me see that wallet."

"What wallet?"

Benjamin stretched out his hand. Emmet hesitated, then he handed it to him. Benjamin looked at it briefly, after which he put it in his own pocket.

"I wasn't hooking him, Mr. Lassiter," Emmet said. "I was only taking out enough money to pay for—"

"To pay for what?"

Emmet shrugged.

"For the drinks," he said.

Benjamin looked away.

"You're fired," he said.

"Mr. Lassiter," Emmet protested. "He came here by himself! I didn't bring him here!"

Benjamin had his ear to the door of the other room. The sound of water rushing into the tub was louder now.

"Your check will be mailed to you," he said, without bothering to glance at Emmet.

"It's not my fault!" Emmet cried.

Without answering, Benjamin lowered himself wearily into the purple armchair, turning it so that his back was toward Emmet.

Emmet stood there. He was breathing hard, glaring at Benjamin's back. He said, suddenly, "I don't think so, Mr. Lassiter!"

"You don't think what?"

Emmet clenched his fists. "I don't think that you are going to fire me!"

Benjamin Lassiter slowly swung his bulk around to face him.

"You've been fired," he said in a low deliberate voice.

"No, sir!" Emmet set his jaw. He leaned forward menacingly. "I think you'd better think it over, Mr. Lassiter," he said.

Once more Benjamin turned silently away from him.

Emmet's voice rose.

"Mr. Benjamin Lassiter, sir, Esquire, the Honorable, and so on and so forth: let me just tell you something. You've got a son who gets drunk and who spends his evenings in nigger whorehouses. How would you like the whole damned world to know that?"

From the next room, Benjamin could hear Robert's voice, strenuously objecting to something. Then there was a loud splash, followed by a long agonized bellow. After that there came a series of muffled whimpers.

Benjamin winced, wishing he could shut the sound of it out of his ears.

He turned slowly to face Emmet, who was looking down at him, his legs arrogantly straddled, the muscles of his jaw twitching.

"You're a stupid man, Emmet," Benjamin said.

Emmet opened his mouth to object. But before he could say anything, Benjamin went on in a low, even voice.

"You're stupid because you threaten me through a member of my family," he said. "Offer to punch me in the nose. Try to steal my money. Gun me down. All right. You're asking for a fair fight when you do that. But when you give me a warning that involves my son, I will simply dispense with any civilized rules of warfare and step on you and rub you out under the sole of my shoe like the goddam little piss-ant that you are." He looked up at Emmet's face with open contempt. "Beat it, Harry Emmet," he told him. "Start running. Get the hell out of my city."

Emmet stared at him for a moment, his face suffused with rage. Then he swung swiftly around and went out of the room, slamming the door behind him.

For a long time after that Benjamin sat staring at the wallpaper, too wrapped in his own thoughts even to notice its bilious color.

The sound of groaning from the next room roused him out of his despondent lethargy. Robert would be needing him now.

He got up and went over to the door.

He listened for a moment.

The deep groans continued. He could hardly endure to hear them. The boy was in pain!

Benjamin opened the door.

CHAPTER FORTY-ONE: THE SWEDISH TREATMENT

Robert was slouched in a chair. He was covered from his neck to the floor in blankets. As he groaned in pain, Brian, standing behind him, was kneading his fingers into the muscles of his neck and shoulders.

"What in God's name are you doing to him now?" demanded Benjamin, looking on, astonished, from the doorway.

"The third step," Brian informed him cheerfully, kneading away. "This is what is known as the Swedish treatment. I took lessons in this from a friend of mine, Timothy Dineen of County Clare. Timothy learned it from a Swedish man who was a professor in it. Now this Timothy Dineen, he was the kind of man you don't run across in the course of every day. He was a one-eyed fellow who sailed into the Skagerrak in the winter looking for herring. He'd come home smelling so bad it would drive you demented. But he had a fine education for all that. Oh," he added, looking up and grinning at Benjamin, "you can't say enough for education, now, can you?"

Hortense reappeared just then. She nodded at him from behind Benjamin's shoulder.

"Did you bring all them ingredients?" he called out to her.

"Every last one!"

"There's a table in there behind you. Set them all down on that, will you, me dear?"

"Sure thing."

She backed away out of Brian's line of sight. They shouted back and forth at each other, from room to room, while Benjamin remained in the doorway between them.

"Got it all, have you?" Brian called.

"Yes, sir!"

"First of all, I want you to separate the whites of the eggs from the yolks. Can you do that?"

"Glad to, Mister."

"That's the girl!" While he spoke, Brian went right on pummeling Robert mercilessly. Now and then Robert raised his head and emitted a bellow of pain and protest. Benjamin, from the doorway, swiveled his head from Brian to Hortense, and back again, observing both operations with a look of utter incredulity.

Hortense glanced up from her egg-breaking.

"Mr. Lassiter, honey. Oh, I'm sorry! I'm sorry. I mean Mr. Lassiter, sir. It's comin' on twelve o'clock, and that's when all those cops is going to come poking around here—"

Benjamin turned to the bedroom.

"How much longer will it take, Brian?" he asked.

"How long is my Aunt Tillie's nose?" Brian snapped back.

Benjamin turned back to Hortense and shrugged his shoulders.

With a deep sigh, Hortense set about breaking and separating the other egg.

CHAPTER FORTY-TWO: LATE ARRIVALS

Hacker had long since, and with his customary unruffled aplomb, served the café brulé, ceremoniously soaking sugar cubes in cognac and lighting them before placing them in the guests' coffee cups.

Now after-dinner drinks were being served.

Mary Lassiter sat in a corner, in a brown velvet wing chair. Ordinarily, she would have reveled at being in the center of her family and their friends, giving full run to her witty mind and sharp tongue. Now she no longer seemed to notice the moments when the conversation flagged in the room. Her eyes were worried and she kept glancing off toward the arched entranceway.

Suddenly, her face was alert again. She had heard the doorbell chime.

Her chin lifted. Her glance traveled across the room, toward Hacker.

Hacker had heard it, too. In fact, he was already on his way to answer it. He turned to Mary with a nod and a reassuring smile. She nodded back to him. And then he disappeared into the hallway.

Mary sat upright in the wing chair, leaning on her cane.

The look on her face spelled both fear and expectation. She did her valiant best to ignore the treacherous fluttering of her heart.

And then her body abruptly seemed to sag and the look of bright and tremulous expectation faded.

"Giorgio mio!" Fawn's voice called out in a penetrating shriek of welcome.

Giorgio Bellonci stood on the threshold of the living room, tall and handsome and very aware of himself in his white tie and tailcoat. Hacker was behind him.

Fawn sailed across the room, a flamboyant streak of vivid red chiffon, and grasped both his hands in hers.

"Everybody," she cried, "this is Giorgio Bellonci, my marvelous teacher. Giorgio, this is everybody."

"She didn't need him to teach her to put on an operatic performance," Emily muttered to Trevor. Trevor only laughed.

And now Fawn was piloting the late arrival about the room.

"This is mother, Giorgio!"

He bowed over Mary's hand and kissed it.

"I am charmed, Mrs. Lassiter," he said.

Mary surveyed him appraisingly.

"You are a very handsome man," she said at last. "Do you sing as well as teach?"

"Ah, Signora," he replied, "we teach only when we are no longer capable of singing!"

Fawn pulled him away.

"And my sister, Rosamond!"

As he kissed Rosamond's hand he looked up into her flushed face.

"This is your sister?"

Stung, Rosamond gave him a faint smile. "You don't see any resemblance, Mr. Bellonci?"

"Now that you speak, signorina," he answered with quick gallantry, "I can *hear* the resemblance!"

Rosamond turned away.

"Now I want you to meet the rest of us," Fawn insisted, dragging him off.

"He must be Neapolitan," Mary declared, watching as he was led up to, and past, the Brodericks and Marvin Malloy. "He can't possibly be a Roman, not with all that charm!" And then she dismissed him for the moment from her mind and looked down at her watch. Where was Robert? And Benjamin? What was keeping them so long?

And now Fawn had led Giorgio up to Emily and Trevor Bullock, introducing him as absolutely the most marvelous voice coach she had ever had.

There was a ragged series of how-do-you-do's.

"We met an Allegra Bellonci in Florence, before the war," drawled Emily. "She was married to some Conte—or was it a Marchese? What was his name, Trevor?"

"The Florentine Belloncis are very rich," Giorgio said. "I have never met them," he added laconically.

Trevor was looking vaguely puzzled. " 'Voice coach,' did you say, Fawn?" he asked. "I'm afraid I don't quite understand."

"How could you possibly, Trevor? It had nothing whatever to do with the stock market," she shot back at him over her shoulder as she tugged Giorgio toward Maude and Richard Palmer.

"And this," she announced, "is my sister Maude and her husband, Richard Palmer. I forgot to ask, Richard dear. How are all the little ones?" She turned to Giorgio. "They have hundreds and hundreds of children!"

"No," Richard replied seriously. "Just four."

And now Fawn suddenly caught a glimpse of a figure standing framed in the doorway.

Her mother had also seen him at the same time. She suddenly sat erect again, her eyes fixed on him.

"Now," said Fawn, dragging Giorgio away from the Palmers, "come and say 'Hello' to my father!"

Benjamin stepped into the room.

"My father," Fawn explained in a voice which carried all the way across the room, "has taken French leave of us all night. It was very rude of him, of course, but he had to go see the Governor, or something, and tell him how to spell his name. Daddy, this is—But you've already met!"

"Indeed!" said Giorgio.

"Yes, indeed!" Benjamin said perfunctorily. His eyes raked the room until they found Mary. Then he smiled at her.

She was leaning forward on her cane, watching him expectantly. Then, suddenly, she smiled back at Benjamin.

"Now say 'hello' to my brother Robert!" Fawn cried.

Robert came in from the hall and stood beside his father. He looked pale and worn, but it was apparent that he was sober.

Mary beamed. Her whole face lit up. She was ecstatic with relief.

"Robert, this is my very dear friend, Giorgio Bellonci!"

They shook hands.

"How do you do?" Robert said.

"I am so very much pleased to meet you!" Giorgio said.

"Excuse me for a minute," Robert said. He left the group and advanced toward Mary's chair.

"Hello, Mother," he said.

She ran her appraising eyes over him. He looked worn and ashen, she thought, as though he had been through some ordeal. Never mind, she told herself. He's home and he's safe. That was all that mattered. She reached up and adjusted the wilted rose in his buttonhole.

He bent down to kiss her.

"I'm sorry to be late," he said.

CHAPTER FORTY-THREE: TWO CLUBS

Several days after the Lassiters' dinner party, shortly after noon, the black Packard limousine drove up Commonwealth Avenue. It came to a halt in front of a large, early Victorian building.

This was Benjamin Lassiter's club.

It was not one of the old established clubs of Boston. In spite of his money, and his house on Louisburg Square, there was no question of Lassiter being admitted to one of them. So Benjamin had been one of the leading spirits in the founding of this one. It lacked, to be sure, the Brahmin luster and the patina of long tradition which the others possessed as their undisputed right. However, it was much more opulent. And there was no questioning the fact that the food was considerably better.

From behind the driver's seat of the limousine emerged Brian Mallory, resplendent in a brand new chauffeur's uniform. He went briskly to the rear door and opened it.

Marvin Malloy was the first to step out. He offered a hand to Benjamin Lassiter. Robert was the last to emerge.

Robert was thinner and paler than he had been on the night when he had made his unwelcome appearance at

Hortense's brownstone establishment, and there was a curious tentativeness to his movements. But at least, as his father observed with a glance of satisfaction, he was moving on his own two feet.

After Benjamin had exchanged a few words with Brian, and three men went up the steps and went through the front doors of the club.

Brian got back into the car and drove away, back to Beacon Hill.

The three men, meanwhile, crossed the marble floor of the entrance hall. They laid their hats and coats on the cloakroom counter.

"Brian's going to turn out all right, after all," Benjamin said to Malloy. He frowned thoughtfully. "There's only one thing about him that bothers me."

"What's that, Mr. Lassiter?"

"Who does he remind me of?" he said.

"You'll think of it, Mr. Lassiter," Malloy said reassuringly.

"Yes," Lassiter said. "Eventually. But meanwhile, it's driving me crazy!" He shook his head. "Well," he remarked, "we might as well go into the dining room."

The dining room looked out onto the trees and the quiet traffic of Commonwealth Avenue. It was a large room with an enormous luncheon buffet set up against one wall. The headwaiter greeted them with marked deference.

"I have your usual table for you, Mr. Lassiter," he said.

The men went over to the buffet table and took their plates. As they moved along, Robert gestured toward the food he wanted and Benjamin filled his plate for him.

"Good afternoon, Mr. Lassiter," the attendant behind the counter said. "What can I get you?"

"None of this stuff," Benjamin said. "You know what I want you to fix me, Barney."

"Steak tartare, Mr. Lassiter?"

Benjamin nodded.

"I'll send it over to your table, sir."

"Good, you do that." He turned back to Malloy. "He's an opportunist, of course, but what's wrong with that?"

Malloy looked puzzled.

"Who? Barney?"

"No. I'm talking about Brian. I'll tell you something, Marvin. The only people worth a damn, the only ones I like, are the takers. The givers are all right. We need them to keep the religions going and the charities, and all that. But the ones who make the whole damned world go around are the takers. The rest of the world would stand still if we didn't have the guys who keep grabbing all the time." He paused. "Well," he said, surveying the room, "I guess we're ready to sit down and eat."

At the moment when Benjamin, with Robert and Marvin Malloy in his wake, was making his way to his usual table, a taxicab was pulling up to the curb of a smaller but extremely dignified mansion in the Federal style, several blocks further up Commonwealth Avenue.

Hacker and O'Hara, both impeccably dressed, stepped out of the taxi. While O'Hara stood on the sidewalk gazing up with awe at the neo-classical façade, Hacker paid the driver. Then Hacker took O'Hara's arm and led him up the steps. O'Hara kept on gaping, regarding every detail of the building. It was almost as though he were being led into a church.

They walked through the door into a quiet, marble-paved entrance hall. They crossed to the cloakroom, where they removed their hats and coats, laying them on the counter with their gloves and scarves on top of them.

"I never thought I'd ever see the day!" O'Hara gasped as Hacker took him by the elbow and guided him along the corridor.

"A club is a club, Mr. O'Hara," Hacker reminded him.

"But the Butler's Club! I never thought . . ."

They had reached the open doorway of the reading room. A tall man with a patrician profile which could have belonged to a Roman senator, stood at the newspaper rack. He removed the London *Times* with its wooden holder. He glanced up at them. His frosty features broke, briefly, into a smile of greeting.

"Good afternoon, Mr. Hacker," he said. His accent was distinctly British—Oxonian, in fact.

"Good afternoon, sir," Hacker replied respectfully.

The man nodded and sank into a leather easy chair.

"Bromfield," Hacker murmured in O'Hara's ear. "He was with the Hallowells for many years."

O'Hara stared at the white-haired man who was now running his hawk-eyes over the columns of the London *Times*.

"*That's* Bromfield!" he exclaimed.

Hacker pushed him down the corridor in the direction of the dining room.

"Composure, O'Hara," he admonished him. "Composure. The first rule! Yes, that was the celebrated Bromfield. He's retired now. He lives in that chair."

The dining room was not a large one. It was beautifully paneled and softly lit. The men at the tables all sat their with an air of being accustomed to being waited on. The conversation was subdued. Not a single voice was raised. Black waiters glided noiselessly among the tables.

The headwaiter had a mirror-black face and a cap of closely cropped white hair. He bowed as Hacker and O'Hara made their appearance.

"Mr. Hacker, sir," he said.

"How are you, Dennison?" Hacker asked affably. "Just two of us."

"Would you like a corner table, sir?"

"Very much," said Hacker.

Dennison led the way to a corner table. As they seated themselves, Hacker said, "Dennison."

"Sir?"

"Waiter number four. One shoe squeaks," Hacker informed him.

"He's a new man, Mr. Hacker. I'll tell him." He moved silently away.

Hacker picked up the menu and leaned back in his chair, surveying the dining room.

"You are sitting in the best run dining room in America," he told O'Hara. "It is kept that way because the membership is encouraged to make complaints."

"I see," said O'Hara, looking eagerly around him.

"It is all a question of detail, Mr. O'Hara," Hacker informed him expansively. "In our profession, there are no such things as trifles. We must notice *everything.*"

In the dining room of the other club on Commonwealth Avenue, Benjamin Lassiter broke off in the middle of eating his steak tartare.

"I don't care what Mulvaney says about the Third District," he told Marvin Malloy. "I'm telling you what to do about the Third District. An extra truckload of turkeys this Christmas and take care of Columbo's boy!"

* * *

By this time Brian had driven the Packard limousine back to Louisburg Square. He pulled up in front of the Lassiter house.

A moment or two later the front door opened and Rosamond ran down the steps. When she reached the car Brian was already at the back door, holding it open for her.

Rosamond got into the car.

"Where shall I take you today, Miss Rosamond?" he asked.

"Out to Brookline," she told him.

He touched his cap and closed the door. Then he went around to the driver's seat.

"Brookline it is, Miss Rosamond," he called through the dividing window. "But you'll have to tell me how to get there."

* * *

In her Back Bay studio, Fawn sat in front of the mirror of her dressing table, powdering her nose.

She paid no attention when the doorbell rang. She merely went on wielding the powder puff. When she had finished, she leaned forward and adjusted a stray curl over her forehead.

The bell rang again.

Unhurriedly, Fawn pushed back the satin-covered bench and stood up. She paused on her way to the door to straighten the floral arrangement on the piano. Then, with a last sideways glance into the mirror and a quick readjustment of the combs in her back hair, she went to the door and opened it.

Richard Palmer stood in the hallway.

For a moment they exchanged expressionless glances. Then Fawn moved back and Richard stepped inside.

* * *

"Turkeys and the pork barrel—that's politics," Benjamin Lassiter was telling Malloy. "Get Columbo's boy into the post office, and Columbo will tell us what's going on in the Third. We've got to find out what's going on behind our backs. We mustn't ever be surprised. That's the fundamental rule, Marvin. It's only the unexpected that can ever defeat us." He waved his fork at Malloy. "So we just make sure by always knowing what is going on in every nook and cranny of the organization."

* * *

O'Hara found it difficult to settle down to eating his lunch. He kept goggling at his surroundings.

Hacker, meanwhile, was taking enormous pleasure in his guest's enjoyment of the occasion.

"You do aspire, don't you, Mr. O'Hara? You *want* to be a butler?"

O'Hara expelled a fervent sigh.

"Oh, Mr. Hacker! What I'd give—"

"Continue to aspire, Mr. O'Hara. Continue to dream," Hacker exhorted him. "And one day I shall be sponsoring you for membership."

O'Hara could only swallow with gratitude.

"When that day comes," Hacker continued quietly, "when you receive, so to speak, your degree . . ." He broke off. "Do you mind my offering advice, Mr. O'Hara?" he inquired.

"Mr. Hacker, I cherish anything you choose to tell me!" O'Hara replied.

Hacker considered.

"Well," he resumed, "the main thing to bear in mind is simply this. The rich are children. All they know is how to play their little games. That's what life is to the rich. It's games, one right after the other. Bounce out of the nursery into the playpen, out of the playpen onto the playground, out of the playground into life. But don't live life, play it. That's the rich for you, O'Hara. Don't you ever forget it."

* * *

Emily Bullock entered the vestibule of a small tenement house in a section of Boston she had never been in before. She drew her furs closer, looking around her with repugnance. How could anyone possibly live in such sordid surroundings? she wondered. Through her own aura of Parma violets she could detect the smell of something distasteful. Then, with a little shrug, she proceeded to climb the rundown staircase.

She paused in front of a battered door on the first landing. The paint was flaking off it. She looked around furtively. A hoarse voice was screaming something from the floor above. She waited. A door slammed and the voice subsided.

Drawing a hand from her muff, she rapped quickly on the door.

It was opened at once by Giorgio Bellonci.

She moved swiftly past him into the room, her eyes at once wary and curious.

With a smile, Giorgio closed the door behind her.

* * *

"But, Mr. O'Hara," Hacker went on, "you must never let them know that they are being watched. You must never let them know that *you* are in control. It's like the birds, Mr. O'Hara. Learn from the birds! I control every moment of their lives. They are no more aware of my manipulating than we are of God. For example, when I notice that the voice of the male is beginning to have a titillating effect on the female, and when you see the female of the species making all those little signs of unrest which betoken the arrival of the mating season, that is the time to act decisively, if you don't want her to lay eggs all over the place and make all kinds of trouble. Do you follow me, Mr. O'Hara?"

"Every word, Mr. Hacker," O'Hara replied reverently.

* * *

The limousine was already beyond the outskirts of the city.

Rosamond sat in stately comfort in the rear.

Brian turned and smiled at her.

Rosamond smiled back.

* * *

Downtown, on Tremont Street, a young girl stood studying the still photographs on display outside a motion picture theater. They were showing William S. Hart in "Tumbleweeds," not that it really mattered to her what the picture was.

She stepped up to the ticket window and fumbled in her bag until she found the money for her ticket.

It was dark when she went inside. She was half-blinded by the quick images flickering onto the silent screen. The piano was thumping away and her heart pounded along with it.

An usher pointed the beam of a flashlight at her feet. She stumbled after him down the side aisle. She slid into a seat in the last row, against the wall.

And now Betsy Bullock sat there stiffly, as though torn between fear and expectancy. She blinked at the screen, not really making out what was happening. She peered down the empty aisle.

Her lips trembling slightly with disappointment, she squinted at her watch. It was past the time. She turned and tried to distinguish the shadows at the back of the house. She was sure now that he had forgotten.

How could he forget?

And then, suddenly, a dark silhouette filled the seat next to hers.

"Harry?" she whispered.

Emmet silently threw his arm around her and drew her toward him in the darkness.

Betsy smiled helplessly, tremulously, into his face.

* * *

"You know where Mulvaney makes his mistake?" Benjamin Lassiter demanded. "He likes to think people are motivated by principles." He laughed harshly. "People are motivated by hunger or by lechery, and if a man accepts that fact early in life, I will put my money on him to make it to the top."

Robert glanced up from his plate.

"Father," he said, speaking for the first time since they had come into the club.

Benjamin beamed with delight that Robert had finally shown a sign of life and was ready to take part in their conversation.

"Yes, son?" he asked gently.

"I just got the answer to something," Robert said, "something that's been bothering you."

Benjamin Lassiter set down his knife and fork. He had already finished his steak tartare. He looked at Robert across the table, puzzled.

"Yes?"

"I know who it is Brian reminds you of."

"Ah. And who *is* it?"

Robert eyed his father full in the face.

"Yourself," he said.

* * *

The Packard limousine was still going toward Brookline. But now Rosamond was sitting up front, beside Brian.

She turned and gave him a hesitant smile.

He kept his eye on the road, but he grinned back at her in the mirror, cocky and triumphant under the visor of his smart new chauffeur's cap.

It was a great country, Brian told himself, and a glorious city with no end to it. And he knew now where he was going.